FOX

MARGARET SWEATMAN

TURNSTONE PRESS

Turnstone Press
607-100 Arthur Street
Winnipeg, Manitoba
Canada   R3B 1H3

Turnstone Press gratefully acknowledges the assistance
of the Manitoba Arts Council and the Canada Council
in the publication of this book.

Cover illustration and design:
Terry Gallagher and Steven Rosenberg, Doowah Design Inc.

This book was printed and bound in Canada by Kromar
Printing Limited for Turnstone Press.

Canadian Cataloguing in Publication Data

Sweatman, Margaret

Fox

ISBN 0-88801-154-7

I. Title.

PS8587.W36F6 1991   C813/.54   C91-097077-7
PR9199.3.S942F6 1991

Excerpts in slightly different form have appeared in
Border Crossings and *NeWest Review*.

I'd like to thank the Manitoba Arts Council for their support.

And I am greatly indebted to Dennis Cooley, Marilyn Morton,
Paula Kelly, Wayne Tefs, David Arnason, Bill Arbuthnot,
my parents, family, and my friends.

Sources are too numerous to mention. Among them:

Salem Goldworth Bland. *The New Christianity*. Toronto: University of Toronto Press, (1920) 1973.

Michael Bliss. *A Canadian Millionaire: The Life and Business Times of Sir Joseph Flavelle, Bart. 1858-1939*. Toronto: Macmillan, 1978.

Rev. (Captain) Wellington Bridgman. *Breaking Prairie Sod: The Story of a Pioneer Preacher in the Eighties, With a Discussion of the Burning Question of To-Day, "Shall the Alien Go?"* Toronto: The Musson Book Company Ltd., 1920.

Mary V. Jordan. *Survival: Labour's Trials and Tribulations in Canada*. Toronto: McDonald House, 1975.

Grace MacInnis. *J.S. Woodsworth: A Man to Remember*. Toronto: The Macmillan Company of Canada Ltd., 1953.

Kenneth McNaught. *A Prophet in Politics*. Toronto: University of Toronto Press, 1959.

Doug Smith. *Let Us Rise!: An Illustrated History of the Manitoba Labour Movement*. Winnipeg: Public Press, 1985.

J.S. Woodsworth. *My Neighbour*. Toronto: University of Toronto Press, (1911) 1972.

For Grant
& for Bailey
& for Hillery

Eleanor's Party

December 22nd, 1918

ELEANOR IS TALL, taller than most men, and her face is long, her thin nose long as a lake-edging highway, her long face and her eyes like almonds, almost, a very strange long woman. She likes her own almond eyes, actually. She says to hell with those fat and innocent faces, my bones, my damn cheekbones anyway, will be fine on my face when it's old. And Eleanor is not old, but she's older than the others, she's old enough now to look like a woman who has been loved. She looks like a big bird, a hawk, a prairie falcon. Glares down from her perch, expectant, distrustful, persistent. Her hands are too big, the fingers splayed, she flings her hands about when she speaks. Her feet are long, she buys her shoes in Chicago, takes the train by herself and stays with a distant relative, and it irritates the old aunts, a single woman alone like that, she's too awkward, she has long since outgrown herself.

She presses into the damp window, the cold fresh as a child, scratches an E for Elaborate in the art nouveau frost. Time, time on my hands. I wish I were sick, I might make myself sick and skip it, stay up here and sulk. The goddam glib gentlemen of St John's. I can't believe I'm having a toboggan party, I'm going to kill Drinkwater, I'd like to poison the whole bloody bunch.

1

It's a shadowless winter day, grim and cold. She stands at her bedroom window, fingering the heavy velvet curtains, burgundy and brocade. She stands at her window and watches the grainy snow lift, indifferent, in the wind, the iron railing, the muddy stubs of yellowed geraniums under a drift of snow in the corner of her balcony. The gnarled elms crack and snap in the cold.

The wide hallway is dark and the smell of baking lifts up the wide stairs and she hesitates on the mezzanine, to listen, to assess, to come out of her dark room where she lives and listens. But she waits too long and when she comes downstairs at last and enters the library where her father has shut them, the toboggan party-people topple about like puppies, she opens the library door upon their yelping and their health.

Drinkwater is beautifully knit. He's telling a funny story, at least everyone's laughing so hard their cheeks must hurt all squint-eyed. Drinkwater puts his blue-sweatered arm about Eleanor, draws her in without stopping his story, and the hello Eleanors don't break the rhythm of his funny tale. Laughter tumbling and harmonious, Eleanor smiling hopefully. Drinkwater is not drinking water, she can smell the warm rum on his warm and sticky mouth. He tips her backward, an extravagant embrace, her rolled hair falling onto the carpet, the roomful of friends hooting and joyful, he says, "Oh! young man, aren't you holding me too close?—Ahh, but my darling, I love you still."

"For christsake Drinkwater." Well who cares anyway, might as well enjoy the dogshow, my yard anyway. And so the party does begin, and it's all right, really. Mary arrives, of course she's late, muffed in fur, probably rabbit.

"How's Aunt Elizabeth?" asks Eleanor.

Mary stops like a fox, gleaming and red, her perfect narrow eyes blue and clear, and Eleanor always marvels at the accuracy of Mary's peripheral vision. Mary answering while she apparently watches Drinkwater, her voice clear and slippery, says, "Sick."

The party is in Eleanor's back yard. Her father's Men have erected a gallows, no not a gallows at all but an ice slide for the toboggans, and they slide all the way onto the Assiniboine River where the Men have shovelled the ice for sliding and for skating. Servants come out with hot chocolate but there's the quick lick of rum in the air, chocolate subterfuge for booze. Wicker chairs have been placed upon a carpet unrolled onto the snow, just an old carpet but the good wool so lovely when it wears bare, and it keeps the ladies' boots dry and their feet are warmed by rocks heated by the bonfire in the stone fireplace at the centre of the lawn where it slopes upon the riverbank. It gets dark early. Then the lanterns are lit and the servants carry trays of roast beef and sweet fresh bread and pickles and cakes. They hadn't even planned to eat outside, but when the evening proved so warm it seemed natural to request that the table be set where the young people can enjoy the calm winter air.

They get moody, these young folk, sitting close about the fire while the night gets thick and the moon a great egg through the elms. Fine young faces round as biscuits, limpid and nostalgic for who knows what. So it does not strike strangely when Melissa McQueen's glassy voice, chill and pure, cuts the hollow chocolate night with a melancholy song from *Lucia di Lammermoor*. And when it's done, and the silence has been sweetened by Melissa's song, no one applauds, it's like a church. And Melissa McQueen knows, she's won them better.

3

Eleanor's Friends

THE PARTY HAS MOVED INSIDE, the ladies have been to the ladies' room where noses have been blown and just a smidgen of powder applied The young gentlemen are allowed to smoke in the library, and this is where they sit for some time, to warm themselves, to enjoy a bit of manly company. But Eleanor is here, and there's nothing much to do about it, it's her house isn't it? Drinkwater perches protectively on her chair. He takes the conversation into the ordinary territory of young gentlemen, just as if Eleanor weren't present. *Suits me fine too, but I wonder how they do talk, when I'm really not here, is it always so ordinary?*

Drinkwater quit university early last spring, saying if he couldn't meet Fritzy on the battlefield, he'd just as soon get out on the commercial battlefield here at home and so on. Drinkwater says we'll need a strong economic foundation to resist the blasts of post-war unrest, and if our lads are going to come home to good jobs and a buoyant future, we'd better get off our butts and perform. So Drinkwater has got himself a fine parcel of land in Crescentwood and he's out marching the commercial district in the hopes of getting some of the older establishment types to invest and he's certain he can make this development go, because just look at the housing starts before the war and before the goddam Panama Canal stole our thunder, but by lord we can get back to the good days it just takes some spunk and all the old money's just got scared that's what and they need a kick that's what they need.

Dwight Scott stands up and stretches lanky by the fire and says he'd better go get his date before she crowns him. Victor Anderson and Bill Popp start ribbing him about how he's all lallygag over Frances Matheson and how he showed off at hockey last night because Dwight and Vic and Bill are the top players in the scrub league at St John's. St John's has three teams, the "Bolsheviki," the "Socialists," and "The Enemy Aliens," and Vic, Bill, and Dwight helped carry off the shaving mug in the last tourny. They're really nifty skaters and top students too.

Eleanor has never heard about this scrub league before. She never went to university, but she might go study abroad now that the war is over. She asks Dwight to tell her the names of the hockey teams again, it feels so strange, hearing these bullish young men say *Bolsheviki* in the library. DW, always observant, says something obscure about Eleanor turning *Red*, and how *Red* will look pretty garish what with all the royal purple and the velvet and the fur Eleanor's so fond of. Typical. Eleanor wishes they could all stop being so goddam funny for a minute because she's been hearing some talk and reading the Trib a bit, and there's been a lot in the papers these days about the Alien and the Bolsheviki threat. But Drinkwater pulls her out of her big chair and says they're all going downtown to the Alhambra to dance. There's a syncopated Broadway jazz band playing and it's time for all good gentlemen to warm their cars. Eleanor pulls DW aside as they're leaving, though, and she says, "What's going on, Drinkwater, I want to know." And Drinkwater, wrapping his blond throat in a white silk scarf, even pauses as if he is serious, kisses her and, ever-gallant, says, "Eleanor, in one year I'll be a millionaire, I promise you. And then I'm going to marry your cousin Mary, and I'm going to be happy happy happy and you know why? Because I will always leave the politics to my servants."

5

The Unlawful Assembly

SUNDAY AFTERNOON, DECEMBER 22nd
WALKER THEATRE
F.J. DIXON, M.L.A.
W. HOOP   R.B. RUSSELL
GEO. ARMSTRONG   S. BLUMENBERG
REV. W. IVENS
Fight for Liberty!

LIKE A FOREST IN AUTUMN, the colours of wood and sunburnt leaves, windy, the pellmell voices of the crowd gabble and crow, men mostly, every seat in the place full, men in the aisles and men in the lobby, with all the clamour of an orchestra tuning, they fill the big room, voices hum and rumble from the front of the stage to the balcony, and above, the restless and baroque ceiling of the Walker Theatre. Russell and Ivens and the others are already on stage, hands in their pockets, talking fast and earnest, and smiles everywhere, Blumenberg telling something funny to Bobby Russell, Russell even cracks a smile, lays his hand on Sam's elbow.

John Queen the Alderman calls the meeting to order and everybody settles down. Up front, a short chubby fellow with a face like a bowl of porridge takes out a notebook, licks his pen. It could've gone sour right then, but nobody takes it seriously, just goodnatured and one guy gets a good laugh when he says in a loud voice he'll correct the spy's spelling when he's done.

Then Bill Hoop takes over, sets fire to the whole bunch of them with his talk about the war and how the world has become a violent place but it's property that's oppression, the end of property means the end of the labour movement's slavery. Stand up, Mr. Charitinoff, says Bill, stand up. Charitinoff lifts a little out of his chair and Bill says, This is the man the capitalists want to call a criminal. Know why? Stand up Mr. Charitinoff—but Charitinoff doesn't want any more trouble he'd like to sit down he shouldn't even be here with bail posted so high and his wife so terrified of the soldiers.

Now the Government is putting men in jail for circulating literature. They want to keep us at war with the German people, the Austrians, Roumanians, the Czechoslovaks, the Poles. Why should we fight? *We have a glimpse of a world just a little beyond, beautiful, and full of hope.*

Sam Blumenberg gets up, says, The Tribune won't name my nationality, he says, well I guess it's entirely unnecessary since my face is the map of Palestine and I sneeze through the mount of Zion.

Sam says he's afraid of criticizing the Canadian Government, he doesn't mind admitting it, he's afraid of going to jail, who wouldn't be? But something's got to change, there's no progress without protest. 1917 was a very good year, for the Capitalists, a golden year. Never before has there been so much money in circulation. And never before so much poverty.

An informal meeting, the speakers most of them standing, climb the podium and stand beside each other, look like vaudeville, look like they'd sing a duet if they knew each other's words and they nearly do. George Armstrong joins Sam, says, During the war Canada's wealth doubled, *more* than doubled, during the most destructive period in the world's history. Why would the ruling class want it to stop?

7

And Bobby Russell says capitalism can't function now that the war's over, there's too many people to employ and too much surplus.

And Sam asks the crowd to unite, he says the returned soldiers and the farmers and the workers must unite and overthrow the capitalist system.

And Bobby Russell prophesies the end of capitalism. And Sam says, People think the Bolshevist is a dark hairy foreigner with a knife in his mouth, a torch in one hand, and a bomb in the other. Then how come a man like that gets a 6-hour 12-dollar day?

Chairman Queen calls for three cheers for the Russian Revolution. Long live the working class! Long live the Russian Soviet Republic! Long live Karl Liebnecht!

After that they try like hell to cable a message of congratulations to the Bolsheviki in Soviet Russia.

January 30th, 1919

Comrade,

I see the Duke of Devonshire is reported in last night's paper as saying that "Bolshevism requires dark and hidden places in which to flourish, and if taken in time, it can be outrooted." If his statement is true, the actions of the authorities in attempting to drive us to dark and hidden corners is entirely in our best interests.

Yours for Socialism

RBR

p.s. Love to Emma and the wee girls.

The Date

Sunday, January 24th

MACDOUGAL IS PECULIAR for many reasons, one of them being his resistance to the automobile. Eleanor's father had warned her at dinner that she'd probably be picked up in a buggy and to wear a lot of clothes. So she put on the blue wool dress with the bit of lace—it makes her look older, but it's freezing outside. She's getting another cold sore on her lip, she knows it, there's that hot little bump on her mouth. MacDougal bangs at the big front door and is talking to her father in the dark front hall, their voices secret, soft. The Generals, says Eleanor to her cat, they are speaking on my behalf. Big of them.

This is An Honour for Eleanor, to be taken to a meeting by her father's friend MacDougal. She feels her hand on the bannister, enjoys for the millionth time the way the mahogany of the wainscotting slows the lamplight, enjoys the dark oil painting of her grandfather, the wool rugs, the reluctance of her skirts trailing the carpeted stairs. And she forgets her own murmuring voice when she sees MacDougal; she feels the undeniable desire to cooperate. MacDougal's age is somewhere between Eleanor's and her father's, 40 something. He is her father's socialist friend, the single socialist.

He takes her arm and he guides her to the buggy, lifts her in, she gets snow on his dark coat, white on dark blue wool, and she laughs and apologizes. MacDougal is kind, distracted. He wears a muskrat hat, his face dark and angular. Eleanor tells him she prefers the buggy, the winter night is surprisingly tender, she isn't cold, the furs are so heavy, warm. MacDougal listens, eyes on the horses, amused by his friend's young daughter, the solemn chatter.

MacDougal is consistently silent with Eleanor, and it is only from her father that she knows anything about him. When he does speak to her, she is so grateful and answers at such length that MacDougal withdraws again into that bemused silence. He seems to enjoy listening to her; he watches her speak, but he watches as if he's in another room. She tells him a story about herself and her friend Grace losing control in church, she and Grace laughing and choking and weeping with laughter and eventually leaving by the door where the choir emerged and all because the minister had been ranting from that ugly book of Isaiah all morning for God's sake! On and on and on about the burning and confounding and the slaves and these naked captives these Egyptians strung up I guess and Woe and Woe and Woe and Grace and I are starting to laugh but then he gets to the part about the women, and that's the end of Grace for certain her nose starts running and the poor old daughters of Zion are going to go bald! and God's going to take all their jewellery! and these women, sticking their necks out all tinkling and mincing until the Lord God burns them up. Well Grace is completely out of control and it feels marvellous, walking out, and they just go on burning up the daughters and then go back to their bloody swords and purge their enemies and everybody.

When MacDougal laughs, Eleanor feels every breath of pleasure in the night, his smile such a contradiction to his face. She asks him where the meeting is to be held and he seems cheerful suddenly and says, "Near Wolseley, thank God, at my friend Bill's. The speaker is an Englishman, have you read any of the pamphlets I left at your house?"

Eleanor has read them. Sitting in her father's wood and leather den, at her father's redwood and brass desk, reading about Revolution, and her father had come in and said, "Poor MacDougal. That bloody nonsense will kill him."

"My father thinks you're an anarchist," she says.

MacDougal doesn't respond, which is typical, and finally irritating to Eleanor, and she's even grateful to feel this irritation. She feels a moment of peace. He has stopped outside a comfortable house on a dark street, lambent light behind lacy curtains, a sleeping porch, screened, a shovelled walk. She should know, she should know nothing, and she's going out with MacDougal, with her father's blessing or manipulation. She hurries up the walk, aware of MacDougal's fast step behind her, chased up the walk and into the warm light of the house on Wolseley Avenue. And a room full of men, it seems very large men with large voices and heavy wit. They are laughing and seem to be telling a collective story, playing upon the same story, elaborating on it till it's chewed to death and spit out on the Persian rug. They are introduced to Eleanor and return her chilled little handshake condescendingly, playacting for a child. The guest speaker is in the dining room. Eleanor can see only his legs, crossed, and his brown laced shoes, he prods the air with his brown foot and responds to the appraising questions of the large young men around him at the dining-room table. The air is full of smoke. All the fierce young men smoke vigorously, standing on their toes, hands in pockets, brows knit with the contracted effort of apprehending the revolutionary speaker from England.

Bill calls the meeting to order. Eleanor is provided with a love seat upholstered in yellow damask. The young men arrange themselves here and there, many on the floor. There is one other woman in the room, widow's black, bland features, flaky skin on her face, wrinkled and probably not much older than Eleanor. A dog wanders into the room, nose to nose with the young men, breaks wind and is ushered out. Eleanor is so uncomfortable she thinks something might collapse, her heart or her mind or her back.

The speaker is middle-aged, tall, lanky, long greying hair, a horsey face and no eyelashes, something's missing. He has a huge voice, "Big Pipes." He tucks his thumbs into his vest, and he asks questions. "Does the miner beneath the mountain gain by the invention of the diamond drill? Does the machinist gain by the machine? Does the labourer gain by his labours? Have you no imagination?" (And Eleanor understands, she has none.) "We are lost in a sea of sorrow, face to face with people dying of hunger, our friends, brothers, comrades murdered, their mutilated bodies left to rot on the barricades. Do the cries of pain not reach you? Is the fabric of your life so soft" (he looks at Eleanor) "so tempting, that you forget, and forgetting, sink downwards into that selfish lethargy which is the breeding place of capitalistic iniquity?"

The words! Eleanor is staring at her hands, they lie on her wool dress, blue, and the love seat is the colour of sun and gold, and around her, the world which she sees in periphery, dark, the diminishing smoke, the heavy men, their leather belts, their breathing. How can they breathe under these words? Eleanor is wondering how to give it all and where to give it. What is this transformation? How can she have missed it? Her brother is dead. She hadn't had the wits to blame anybody, and it's her fault, she is so stupid!

"You poets, painters, musicians, if you understand your true mission and the very interests of art itself, come with us. Show the people how hideous is their actual life, and place your hands on the causes of its ugliness. Fire the hearts of the people with glorious revolutionary enthusiasm. And then, and only then, will you lead a complete, a noble, a rational existence."

The young men applaud in the little house and stub out their cigarettes, such is their enthusiasm. There is the hearty shaking of hands, the earnest talk. Eleanor remains seated and the young men tower over her, she feels like pulling her legs up under her, disappearing into her long skirt. It is impossible. Has she ever met a poor person?—there is the washerwoman and sometimes she brings her little girl with her, a tiny thing, what is that odour of poor people?

13

How can she give all her money away? She doesn't *have* any money, her friend Grace doesn't have any money, her cousin Mary doesn't have any money, it is all their fathers' money and they say they've earned it and maybe they have too. Private property? Take it, she has none. But oh to burn with revolutionary enthusiasm!

Then MacDougal comes to get her, takes her by the hand and she willingly becomes the little girl, led from the noisy house, wrapped in her fur coat, helped into the buggy, and driven into the night by MacDougal. There is another meeting, it's at Market Square, another socialistic meeting, MacDougal tells her, not looking at her, driving the horses quickly down Portage Avenue.

A large crowd has gathered at Market Square. They are quiet, stand around waiting for the speaker, talking to each other, a rumpled bunch of men, labourers and immigrants. She sits in the buggy, withdrawn into herself, watching the crowd. She is frozen with something like embarrassment, the feeling of paralysis that came over her at the Wolseley house, her face hurts from its own immobility. MacDougal ignores her, he's listening in the other direction. Down from Main Street come the lighted torches and men on horseback, uniformed men, and they're shouting all the old slogans, Bolshevikis! Go back to Russia! All of it's been in the Tribune. Eleanor hates the repetitive chants, she begins to feel the old dread, her familiar nightmare alight at the back of her mind when she recognizes the soldiers' hatred, Huns! Prussian aliens! The stupid curses, she isn't sure she's awake, there in her wool and fur.

The soldiers ride into the crowd at Market Square and chase the men on foot, men run into alleys and doorways, some of them running silent, and Eleanor feels an entirely new sensation when she recognizes the terror. The uniforms march off toward Smith Street and MacDougal follows, biting his lips, avid as a spectator at a rugby match. He follows the crowd to an office on Smith Street and then there's the breaking of windows and someone sets fire to papers inside, throwing burning papers out the windows, a desk comes sailing out of an upper storey window, horses are dancing and the soldiers sing their chorus, repetitive and raw, Hun, Alien, Bolshevik. And then, Jew! Blumenberg! They want a man named Blumenberg! North. To the dark north end and Samuel Blumenberg's office. The Bolshevik Jew! British justice! And then somewhere, deep in someone's stomach at the fringes of this cavalry, choking laughter.

Even still, MacDougal turns the buggy around as if he's going to follow the hunters on their scourge of the north end, but something in the trotting pace of his team recalls him, something in the gentility of Eleanor's lacy throat breaks the pace, the laughter moves like broken glass to the foreign territory of the north end. And MacDougal turns around again, they ride back down Broadway, back to the river, they cover the bridge with the graceful measure of their trotting horses, down to the Crescent, up the semi-circle of Eleanor's father's drive, returned to the heavy walnut door. Eleanor is so tired she can't look at MacDougal. She is clumsy getting down from the buggy, trails a fur rug into the slush on the drive and throws it, jerky, back onto the seat beside him. MacDougal is watching without compassion, staring at Eleanor's stiff retreat, waiting for the eternity it takes the maid to answer Eleanor's knock. Eleanor standing at her father's doorstep, her shoulders folded around her, yearning for her own disappearance into the house, up to her room, the elegance of her own room the evidence of her own useless stupidity.

Canada Must Be British

THE GROCER HAS DELIVERED the bread and bacon, the dairyman has delivered the milk and eggs, the newsboy has tossed the morning edition, and the pale winter sun has made its cameo appearance between the homes on the opposite side of the park. An insular city on a mild winter morning.

It is a quarter past eight.

Mary has been reading Henry James. Late last night, she was reading by the fire in her room. When she heard her father come in, she was positive it was after two. And this morning, while she lay in the pocket of dark waiting for the winter day delayed by solstice, she heard his precise step on the hardwood margins of the hall. It must have been before six when he left the house.

Something has gone wrong.

She is unaccustomed to fatigue, and she wonders if the pain in her head, like the pinch of bobbypins, is the harbinger of flu. She knows that she owes it to herself to be rested and well. But her lids rub like whetstones upon her restless eyes when she shuts them to sleep, and her little tongue flutters against her teeth like a bird panicking in the verandah.

She is plainly overwrought.

She goes to her father's room, takes from the coatstand his maroon smoking-jacket; it is warm and smells of gingersnaps; it wraps her comfortably, and it looks quite rakish over her silk pyjamas. Mary always moves *legato*, a ballerina between poses. Yes, she is like a ballerina in a company, one of the lovely maids upstage, pointing her pink toes rather listlessly, languorous, accepting no responsibility for the extravagant arabesques of the principal dancers. In this fashion she strays from her father's rooms, through his dressing room, to the steamy marble bathroom, and into the dark camphor-sweetened sick room where her mother lies calm as a lily, Mary's beautiful mother pressed upon embroidered sheets, white crocheted comforter, white hair loose upon the pillow, and her hands, folded one upon the other, white hands, bruised, the plum-coloured shadow fed by the rhythm of her heart. Mary sits beside her mother on the edge of the bed and takes her wrist to test that stubborn pulse. Her mother's eyes are shadowed and watching Mary's reluctant touch.

"What will you do today darling?" asks her mother.

"Nothing much. Maybe go out."

"Would you do me a favour then?"

Mary waits. She will promise, ardently, to do anything her mother asks, and it will take the entire day to convince herself that whatever her mother has requested is impossible, really, and would serve no purpose after all, there's no point is there, what are servants for?

"There was trouble last night, for your father, at the plant. He's very upset."

"I know. I heard him."

"Reverend Bateman is coming to the house this morning. To see your father, but he won't be here. You must receive him. You see, I can't today, I can't get up, I'm sorry."

"Reverend Bateman? The one with eczema?"

"Has he? He's sour as a gooseberry, I admit. I'm nearly grateful to be stuck in bed today."

"Why's he coming here then?"

17

"Haven't any idea. I imagine when he learns Rodney's not at home, he'll drink his tea and tell you you're a good little woman and then he'll go away."

"Do I have to talk to him Mum?"

"Lord no. Just listen."

The Old Flag

He's clearly disappointed to have come for nothing, but when the Reverend (Captain) Wellington Bateman sees the charming Mary present herself in the drawing-room, well, he might stay for a cup of tea. A scone would be very nice, very nice indeed. Eyeing Mary, stirring three sugars in his little cup (Spode), the Reverend (Captain) Wellington Bateman's nose drizzles a little and he sniffles politely. The Reverend has very advanced ideas, some in his congregation would say, very advanced ideas on the education of women. And he thinks, well she's obviously British, that's a British complexion and there's a sterling quality to her, could only come from a British home. So there is no sense sitting in silence with a pretty British girl. She can hear, can't she? She has sense and the fine moral fibre of her race, doesn't she? Well?

The Reverend begins with a eulogy for the Fathers and Brothers and Sweethearts who sleep in Flanders and France. Mary is very quiet and tranquil, her obedient little head warms the Reverend's heart, an easy task; the Reverend's heart is a hot-water bottle wrapped in a Union Jack. So impressed is he by Mary's obsequious posture, he chooses to entrust to her the import of the serious matters he has come to discuss with Sir Rodney.

The Burning Question of To-Day

Last night, I attended a meeting in honour of a dead German named Karl Liebknecht. It is sufficient to tell you my dear, I have never before witnessed such a desecration of the British flag. I stood where I had a view of hundreds and hundreds of faces, and in "plain mug" profile, I could see the second and third and fourth editions of Hindenburg, Ludendorff and Von Kluck. And whenever the soap-box orator lambasted the government, or incited the aliens to "Revolution," the Huns were on hand to howl their approval.

Well, it is a blessed mercy our boys were there to set things right. Just as the fun began, the soldiers made a rush for the firebrands. "Fritzies are all the same to us!" they cried. The Socialists fled in terror. The Soldiers overtook them. The Socialists attempted to take refuge in the Austro-Hungarian Club. Our boys smashed it entirely. The aliens fled to the German Club on McGregor Street. Again, we smashed them right proper, and the windows of ten or twelve other buildings owned by Germans and Austrians, completely demolished.

You are not perturbed by this? It's warm in here isn't it? Call the manservant to let in some air. You're pale, winter air is not to be depreciated of its medicinal value. How is your poor mother? In my discomfiture, I quite forgot to inquire. So ill? God's will be done.

Your father departed early this morning. Yes, I'm not surprised. You don't expect him for dinner. You know, I'm half-tempted to wait. While I do not presume to second-guess Sir Rodney, still, it would not surprise me to see him home this forenoon.

Let me put it to you in bold terms. You are a young woman of understanding, yet I do not expect you to comprehend thoroughly the gravity of these matters. Listen closely. Your father has in his employ some four or five hundred aliens, Germans and Austrians among them. Do you expect, after last night's demonstration of Kaiserism, they will have the temerity to report to work this morning? Perhaps this will bring the point home: today is Monday isn't it? It is washing day. And has your woman arrived to perform her duties?

Who Are These People?

A Limey, a Scot, and a Frog catch a Hun, and they want to kick his arse before they send him back to camp. So across the way there's this henhouse and in the henhouse, there's this skunk. This henhouse stinks like trench rot. So the Limey, the Scot, and the Frog, they decide to put it to the test. Right? So the Limey goes first. And alls he can stand is five minutes and he comes out again. So the Scotchman takes his turn—and he stays five minutes and out he comes. Then the Frog goes in and he stays five minutes and comes out. Last of all they send in the Hun—and he stays fifteen minutes— and the skunk comes out!

**GYPSY WEDDING
ALMOST HALTED
BY RED SCARF**
Policeman Believes Carmine
Headgear is Anarchist Symbol
Winnipeg Tribune

MACDOUGAL DIDN'T SLEEP LAST NIGHT. Not one bit. He thought he would but he didn't. That's all right, sun's up now. MacDougal decides to go downstairs and work.

He flips the doorsign to OPEN and sits himself down with his ledger. It will be a cold and sunny day, a perfect day to write, warm and bookish in the blinkered light of his office. He rubs his sand-scratched eyes with his clean hands, passes his clean hands over his stubbled chin, and stumbles over the memory living in his heart and his liver, the nearly visceral memory living under the soap. Decay. A mattress in a room full of hungry kids. MacDougal nuzzles his nose in his hands now, the kids have clawed the plaster in patches, out of the wallpaper that was English periwinkles. Seems every time he gets tired, his own body exudes this smell, a smoky damp smell of rot.

MacDougal has acquired Poverty the way some people acquire God. His own family was wealthy, by old country standards. His father had been a woollens manufacturer in Lanark, until he sold his mills and came to Canada to be a Methodist minister in Ottawa. The old man had become stranger, and darker, and more pessimistic, in the years of MacDougal's adolescence, dying resolutely of blood poisoning caused by his own rotting teeth.

It was his father's peculiarities that made the church an attractive career for MacDougal, who saw it as a difficult solution, a place in which he might dissolve, rid himself of his inauthentic memory. As an attractive young minister, MacDougal had moved quickly through two wealthy congregations, one in Ottawa and one in Toronto, dismissed from both for his humourless sermons on the New Christianity, and for his relentless and unseemly passion for contradiction.

So he is resting, here in Winnipeg. And writing his great prophetic history of social reform. He is in hiding, in his bookstore. And writing sulphurous columns for the Labour News.

There's a glass-rattling rap on the window, the door opens, and in comes this little man, a pink face with a mouth thin as a ray, a bland mean face. He is suited up with good brown wool and a muskrat collar, well-paid well-fed. No smile for MacDougal the shopkeeper, but he has a neat trick: he invites MacDougal's eyes just long enough to suggest they should be smiling and then at that moment, the fat man pulls out, and MacDougal has been rejected despite himself. So MacDougal unhinges his patience, discovers yet again that he has an abundance of the stuff.

The little man walks carefully about MacDougal's bookstore. They play peek-a-boo about the book stacks, MacDougal amusing himself with the observation that he can see the man's stomach before he sees his face. MacDougal taptaps his pipe on the wastebasket, the little man breezes by Recent Fiction. MacDougal stokes his pipe and lights it, the little man slows down by Theology. MacDougal chews the thick lid of smoke, and through the greywhite filter sees the little man turning slowly, eight frames per second, toward

Social Reform

where he stops. And the satisfied, suspicious-mother look on his face tells MacDougal, this man works for the Government, and this man's father was an Irish store clerk with an appetite for liquor, and this man is going to get a promotion in pay. One cigar-shaped finger pries a thin book by Max Adler out of the case, *Socialism and the Intelligentsia*.

"Would you like to sit down with your book?" asks MacDougal.

He sits, a warm denture smell bellowing out of his mouth when his diaphragm is squeezed by his stomach.

"A recent translation," says MacDougal. "Glad to get it."

They are quiet. A streetcar passing. The man is thumbing through the book, breathing through his nose.

"Sedition," he says finally, placing the book on MacDougal's desk like it weighs a ton. "Who are you working with?"

MacDougal tells him he owns the shop alone, but he knows it's a stupid way to stall this fellow so he asks him his name.

BILL BENSTOCK: DOMINION CENSOR

MacDougal gets this bad-dream feeling, enjoys the cold-gin sense of alarm, and he watches Bill Benstock rolled in his chair like a hungry armadillo sticking a long tongue out to lick the ink from the page.

"I can smell sedition a mile away," says Benstock modestly. "Learned it during the war. Where to look."

MacDougal nearly chokes himself with his pipe. Smoke everywhere.

"Sedition."

"That's right."

"The war's over, or haven't they told you."

Benstock speaks precisely, must write a sharp memorandum. "Yes. But the censorship laws are still in effect."

"Yes, well that is a concern of ours, mine."

Ours.

The Communist Manifesto The Origin
of the Family Private Property
and the State Wage Labour and Capital.
Marx and Engels. Engels and Marx.

"These are books, words on a page."

"Mr. MacDougal, do you know what sedition is? It's a hot word in a dry place."

At great caloric expense, Benstock pries a tabloid out of his coat pocket and places it right side up before MacDougal.

"There's a lot of interest in this literature Benstock, too much for the Government to stop."

"We don't need to stop their interest. We need only to stop you."

Benstock lifts both hands in what looks to MacDougal like a perfectly geometrical gesture. Watching the cathedral shaped by Benstock's hands, MacDougal places his elbows upon his desk and lifts his hands to form a spire of his own. Returned to himself, feels his lungs fill, such a beautiful balance, to have two of so many things, and his voice is his full deep radiovoice, and he says, beautifully, as if he'd written it, he says, "This isn't any continental socialism, you fat idiot. It may not have occurred to you, these are the policies of the opposition party in the British House of Commons."

"But we are here, Mr. MacDougal, in your little bookshop, it is Tuesday and everyone who is willing and able is at work, and those who are not at work are either lazy or looking for someone to blame. And we intend to focus that blame away from the Government, we choose to lay the blame elsewhere, the foreign element will do nicely. Starikoff, Rozaniff, these are Russian names?"

"Things have changed. The people are telling you, things have. Changed."

"The people are damned cattle and you know it. We intend to drive them, to herd them as we wish. Come off it MacDougal, you're no different from me. You've an interest yourself, in moving stock."

Benstock hauls himself out of the chair. He has a voice that MacDougal now realizes is one that can be called "insinuating." He has never heard a voice like this before. Benstock stands over MacDougal, savouring the rare perspective, he says, "Things must be in harmony, in pleasing agreement with the Dominion. And besides, the food tastes like shit in jail."

He makes a superb exit, pulling the door behind him so the wind ruffles the papers on MacDougal's desk, in the absence of the Dominion Censor.

MacDougal locks up after him. Then he steps from his dark store, pushes the screen door against the new snow, to the sunny, snowy back lane. The fact of blue, an empty sky, the brilliant cold sunlight, MacDougal walking blind out the back door of his bookstore.

Making Faces

One Girl Will Surrender
Job To Soldier Boy
Winnipeg Tribune

MARY'S LIPS ARE Nearly Rose. Mary's cheeks are Tender Peach. Mary's skin is Linen and Cream. Mary's eyes are Royal Blue.

Mary's nose is small and delicate. Mary puts it close to the glass. Mary's lashes are so lustrous. They could benefit from a light brush. A light. Brush.

Mary's forehead is smooth and lustrous. Looks much nicer after Cucumber Splash. Mary's fragrance is Eau de Paris. Her décolletage is Faultless and deep. (And a vein the colour of Crocus, slender tissue, steady pulse, from her Chestnut hair to her Ashbrown eyebrow.) She will never grow old, she will never be thirty, she would like to be twenty, forever and ever.

Mary tipples a little sherry. She loves this house when it's sunny and still. Her mother is sleeping or she should be. Mary would like to go to the cinema.

Elsi Ferguson is on at the Gaiety. And Mabel Normand stars at the Majestic. The Dominion is featuring *The Hidden Truth*, but DW wants to see that thing by De Mille. Maybe I'll just check once more on Mother. Mary brushes her Love Match hair.

Mary is wearing a modest gabardine, tailored and belted, dove grey and trim. The little felt hat (with a soft fluted brim) is exactly the shade of her grey suede shoes. She closes the door to her grandmother's wardrobe, studies her back in the full-length mirror. Her waist is slender and her figure alluring. She's learning to smile without spoiling her eyes.

And there is DW at the foot of the bannister. He's never seen Mary so fetching and prim. A woman like that would make all the men envious. And besides her father has splendid connections. She looks at him sweetly, tender, considerate. A woman like that will make him a wife.

They go out in Drinkwater's smart grey roadster. He takes her to the Lyceum to see *Eyes of the Soul*. It's a heartwarming story about a young soldier who's blinded and cynical, bitter and alone. When along comes Elsi Ferguson, nobly compassionate, she loves him, it alters him, she's the light of his life. What happens after that pulls at their heartstrings. And sends them home kinder, and better Canadians.

STRIKE & RIOT INSURANCE

Fire Insurance Policies DO NOT cover any losses caused by strikers & rioters. If a GENERAL STRIKE occurs Insurance will be almost impossible to obtain & rates will be prohibitive. Place your insurance NOW while you can get it.

Ryan Agency Ltd. Insurance, 9th floor Paris Building

Lunch

SHE IS BIG IN THE BONES. A woman like that won't go to fat, but she's heavy boned. She is hungry, she forks the meatpie, golden piece of carrot falls. Peasant's body in rich clothes. She is hungry and she forgets her table manners, hasn't spoken to her companion in how long? Now, she remembers herself, and wipes her mouth. She is accustomed to the feel of Irish linen in her hands, on her mouth. She likes the sweet yellow crust, crumbles pellets of bread with her tongue. With pride she brushes flakes of pastry from her large green velvet lap.

She is accompanied by the little mink her cousin, pert. You don't see the greed in the way the little cousin takes her food, mincing it behind a shapely upper lip, delicate chewing brings out the dimple, fine, petal, she is mauve, a blue belle. God she is small and pretty, and at the centre of her, a spine of 18 karat gold.

They have been at luncheon nearly two hours. They do as they please. Thick hair with hat, pinned. Behind the rich, a mind on food. Here I sit, scribbling at my table with a pipe, occupied. I'll return to the office late. Like a man of business. Competition for sharks and fools, must be larger vision, bring into being a world without cruelty.

See them having their luncheon. Café Mozart, it's a lady-like place. They are not aware of anything, the room, faces, a blue, theatrical backdrop, vaguely a landscape behind the portrait, the important thing, her white neck, its jewel. Trained to keep to themselves. When I present myself at their table, as I leave, it will take her a moment to recognize.

"Eleanor. How are you?"

"Oh, I didn't, have you been here?"

"Just on my way."

"For long? We didn't. This my, Mary, I would like you to meet my friend of my father's, Mr. MacDougal, my cousin, Mary Trotter."

"How do you do? The ladies at lunch. Well I must be off."

"We're off too. There's music this afternoon, I don't suppose you would join us. At a home near, we're just walking from here, no need for a car mild day such as this. Chamber music, you like it despite everything? It's soon, we're just off."

"Thanks, no. I've work to do. Pleased to meet you, Mary. Eleanor. My best to your father."

He walks to the door, turns back. Reapproaches. "I hope you were all right. The other night. I was carried away. You wouldn't have. I apologize."

"No. Don't do that. I enjoyed it. Or no. I was fine, I'm fine now. Thank you."

"Yes."

What Dixon Said

Do we need idealism now? YES! What ideals do we need?
Justice, Liberty, and Love.

ELEANOR'S BROTHER HAS BEEN dead one year today. A year of winter. One year, today. In winter, time stands still.

Grace has come today, though the streets have been blown clean by the blizzard, whited and drifting ghosts of black trees. Grace is Eleanor's closest friend, between them they love Eleanor's dead brother, cherish this love between them like a portrait, polished, a talisman, polished by their breath. Though the city crouches to watch the blizzard blow itself out, Grace has come to see Eleanor, she has burrowed a quinzy through the snow to Eleanor's house, she has been welcomed, to the fire, to the tea with milk and honey, the two women sitting at the low table by the window to watch the wind the wind to watch the wind. And drink tea from China in a Chinese teapot under a quilt sewn there is no doubt by a tiny woman in a house by the side of the Yangtze.

There is always too much to say to one another and it is always important. Analogy is a virtue; the smallest nuance is tremendous as any public event, as sparrows do fall.

There are hermit souls that live withdrawn,
In the peace of their discontent.
There are souls, like stars,
that dwell apart,
In a fellowless
firmament.

They climb the stairs like dizzy children, swaying and bumping shoulders while they talk. They wander through the upper storey, past Eleanor's rooms, to Tony's, and open his door for the first time without knocking. His windows face south and his bedroom is full of snowy light. On his walls are family portraits, and one framed homiletic verse embroidered on linen. They sit on his high soft bed, quiet, it smells like wax in here. Eleanor walks to his dresser, looks at herself in the framed mirror, and then at Tony's trophies. Golf, polo, diving, tennis.

There are pioneer
souls that blaze
their paths where
highways never ran
but let me live
in a house by the side of the road
and be a friend to man.

Tony would have gone to university after the war. He would have studied Law. He would have studied Medicine. He would have studied Theology. "Do you think so?" "Yes," says Grace laughing. "And wouldn't that knock the hat off your dad!" Tony would have left the family business to their older brother in the East. Tony would have been a minister.

Tony would have married Grace. Grace would have had four children. "Six!" "And all of them living." Grace would have been a minister's wife in a house beside a Church. Eleanor looks speculatively at Grace. "Grace," says Eleanor. "You've got money in your bones."

Tony would have studied Law. Grace and Eleanor pull the pillows from his bed, cover their ankles with a throw. And together the two women conjure him through the endless afternoon, Grace and Eleanor chasing the memory of Tony down the lunar streets, faces washed by laughter big with sorrow, remembering, he did do things like that didn't he, no one else ever did things like the things he did. And the times we sat in the stern of the big old steamer on the river all night long and the northern lights and the lights from shore homing us and wondering how far it goes and why it doesn't run perfectly, he was always fond of speculating on the age of things and how it all started and he was kind, always, and handsome, I loved his looks, and his eyes filled up so easy, his goodnature full as a rainbarrel. He would have been 22 next month.

What Ivens Said

We are very proud of our brand new Legislative Building!
YES! It will make a grand home for the Labour Church!

But for now, this afternoon, blizzard or no, the meeting is at the Labour Temple (it won't be long now, the meetings will be held outside under a summer sky though winter lasts forever).
Eleanor's brother has been dead one year today.
There's a congregation warming its hands at the Labour Church this afternoon. Dixon's there. For nearly two hours, he talks. Ivens talks. Robinson talks. The people are sitting with their heads in their hands, their eyes on the floor or the woolcoat back of a friend, their chins on their palms, all ears, *Listening.* And the words stitch their brows, harrow thinkinglines from eye to eye. When a face is full of such listening, it lights up from inside like a piece of paper written by the sun through a lens.
Jesus was a carpenter's son.
Dixon says it's wealth should be conscripted, not just men. The sacrifice of life must be matched by the sacrifice of wealth. And millions of acres of land lie idle in the hands of speculators.
And the waste places of the fat ones shall strangers eat.

And Dixon says, Justice demands that money and mud shall not be more highly regarded than human life. And Dixon says, The government is taking the men it needs, it ought to take the money and the land it needs—but it doesn't.

And Ivens says, Root out the capitalists and let the toilers take over the industries. *It's just a matter of time.* And Ivens says, All you have to do is walk into the factory and tell the owner you are going to take it away from him and the thing is done!

But the police know all about it: *a band of Bolshevist spellbinders, a dangerous crowd of illiterate foreigners.*

Woe unto them that decree unrighteous decrees, and that write grievousness which they have prescribed,

Take it

to turn aside the needy from judgment, and to take away the right from the poor of my people,

Take it

that widows may be their prey, and that they may rob the fatherless! And Lloyd George said and Robert Burns said and Oscar Wilde said and Mr. Shakespeare said and Abraham Lincoln said and Mr. Dooley said, Don't ask f'r rights. Take them.

Now will I sing to my wellbeloved a song of my beloved touching his vineyard. My wellbeloved hath a vineyard in a very fruitfull hill

And he fenced it

mmmm   mmm   mmmm   mmm   mmmm   mmm
    mmm   mmmm   mmm   mmmm   mmm

And Mr. A.J. A— , K.C., said,

I maintain that this so-called Labour Church is merely a camouflage for the preaching of sedition, for fanning the flames of unrest, intended to make you forget all you ever were taught at your mother's knee, to remove the word duty from the dictionary and substitute pleasure for vice. The whole vile doctrine preaches duty to class, self before country.

Winnipeg Tribune

Rent

My sister Aileen, she's got awful circulation. Sometimes early as September, Aileen's hands are turning white from the knuckles down and by November she'll have the frostbite and her fingers turn livid and she says she gets pains in her hands like someone shoving toothpicks up her nails. Keeps her awake.

So tonight after work we walk home, I give her my good gloves to wear over her wool ones but it doesn't do any good anyway. Her boots leak too. I know this cause I seen the way she leaves footprints wet as somebody coming out of the bath, on the floor when she comes home and takes them off after work. She most times walks home to save carfare and her stockings soak through. Every time I see Aileen's wet footprints on the floor it makes me want to puke, like I feel strange toward her. She's the pretty one. But she's cagey, you know.

We both of us work for the T. Eaton Company. Aileen is in the Ladies Wear whereas I'm in the Furniture and that. Lamps and that. Sometimes they put me in the Mothers' Department. And all day long the southend society dames come in like they're the only ones ever had a baby, like they thought the baby up, never screwed nobody for it you know, the kid just popped up during a game of bridge or something.

But to get back to Aileen. It's such a big windy night I think we're nuts to be out but there's hardly nothing to eat at home except what I saved from lunch, some soda biscuits and there's some ham left. I keep a jar of cold water in the icebox, cold water is good for filling you up at night so you can get to sleep. Sunday next we're saving for a bit of meat and that. So we walk home along Main so we can go by the stores and see if there's anything might look good on my sister Aileen. Because the trouble is, the boss expects her to look like a friggin debutante when she's selling the rich bitches their fancy frocks. But there's no goddam way Aileen's gonna spend her entire month's pay on one of them dresses she sells at T. Eaton bless his ass.

So we're walking into this wind that'll freeze your spit before you can shut your mouth, and I'm expecting my sister Aileen to complain about her hands and feet freezing off but she doesn't and so I'm worried right away because she's been quiet like this for a week or two. I mean I know it's too friggin cold to chat but you'd think Aileen'd say something for godsake, like Oh lordy, she says like that, Oh lordy. I mean she's a sweet kid she really is, so that's why what happens tonight is the last straw and I'm out to get Mr. T. Eaton I mean it.

We're walking right smack into the wind coming outta the north. Even in the middle of winter my sister Aileen can look foxy but she freezes her ass off to do it. And it's not out of the ordinary that a Hot Spot slows down and I can see this guy, he's a *gentleman* like, looking across the passenger seat at us, or more exactly at Aileen because she's the looker not me I admit it. Well I says to Aileen, I don't know how you do it honey but you can get lucky out ice fishing for christsake. And I'm counting on her to laugh anyway but she just gives me this look. Her face, and it's so pretty I'm not kidding, thin and those cheekbones like fashion models, like she could be a model I bet. She turns her face to me like this, I get such a chill like somebody splashed me with whiskey when I'm starkers. Empty. Like you could hang a sign on her says Room to Let. She stops. I want her to keep walking to get out of that friggin wind so I turn my back to it and walk backwards down the main counting on her to run to catch up. But Aileen is walking over to this guy's car and he's rolling his window down and they're talking. They talk for a minute. He opens the cardoor, Aileen gets in like that.

Well I'm too cold to stand there and figure it out so I practically run the rest of the way back to our flat that we share, five bucks a month, furnished, sort of.

I can always take a bath, so long as the other tenants in the place don't mind me locking myself in there for half an hour. And I'm just coming out of the tub when Aileen walks in. She just hangs up her coat and takes off her dress. And I know it just looking at her, well it's not that hard to see when somebody's just got laid. Aileen and me been through too much to mince words so I ask her if he gave her anything for it. She puts five bucks on the dresser and she says he screwed her in the back seat, says he had some kind of rug on the seat and it kept them warm. He humped her and then he gave her a lift home. He's scared of getting caught by his wife. He says he's going to give Aileen a ride home once in a while.

And I want you to know, we're talking. It's like now we're together and you don't stand a chance, turn us down, not this time. And it'll be a great day, Mr Timothy Eaton. A great goddam day.

The Canon's Diary

March 21st
and cold as a grave

At last, I have been to the new Church. There was a visitor at the pulpit, a new man from the East. Strange to say, he reminds me of someone, and I can't for the life of me think of whom. I don't warm to the fellow. He has an attitude of discomfort with company, as one who is always formal, even with himself.

His is a nostalgic sort of Christianity, to my mind. "Child at Christ's knee" blah blah. I'd be a child again too, but for this holy pain in my spine.

I want to hear more of this New Christianity. Would be a divine confluence, should the original Christian impulse enter the daily and the political. Would be the flowering of God's will.

That Partridge woman for lunch. Again. Voluble appetite. Like ten men.

Read the Labour News after. In solitude with my faithful pipe. Red News. My boys will be done. There is trouble brewing. The men can't come home to nothing, not with the war still in their blood. Justice. The red run earth.

Dinner

BEFORE THE FIRE HAS BEEN LAID, before the lights have been lit, lies the frozen body of an afternoon, scarred by the branches of the brief blue dusk. Eleanor can't move. She waits at the very centre of the rug where the patterns run most rigorous. It's five o'clock. Coffee tables, candlesticks, footstools, the oak reading desk, the ebony chess set, the oriental firescreen, the bric-a-brac. Distinct in the slab of old winter, these objects, embalmed in light thin as vinegar. Eleanor has been out walking, slipping on good leather soles over the folds and crusts of winter, hobbled by her own clothes, stricken and embarrassed and disconnected from herself at every juncture.

Her cousin Mary had driven by, her man Walter at the wheel, very gay she was, and beside Mary, Emma Partridge whom Eleanor has always liked. Eleanor has invited them for dinner, and Mary has said she'd come if there were men invited too, Drinkwater and MacDougal. So they all will come for dinner, and maybe then, the black dog will retreat.

Eleanor wanders from drawing-room to front hall. The coiled radiators spit and sizzle. There is a silver tray on the bishop's table in the entry. It has been engraved with leaves and nymphs and olives, it sits on three tiny velvet feet, and in it, callers leave their cards. Mostly messages for Eleanor's father. Her green kid gloves lie upon these messages. Eleanor's gloves are very large, her hands have written themselves upon the leather, it is so fine, the gloves in the silver tray full of messages for her father, their palms up.

But here is Drinkwater at last. She surprises him by opening the door herself, she catches him before he has prepared himself for greeting, and she sees, too briefly, his face as it used to be when she knew him as a boy, before he outgrew his sorrow. It is a strange face, Drinkwater's, amused, removed, impassive.

It isn't easy to sit with him. He expects animosity from Eleanor and seems to enjoy it. She takes him into the chill drawing-room. The drawn light doesn't appear to affect him at all. Drinkwater sits, drowsy and contrite as an altar boy with a hangover. He is putting on weight, just on the face, seems swollen with health, his eyes are puffy, his eyelids triangular, mauve, and his eyes blue. He rarely lifts his eyes to anyone, he slides where the conversation runs shallow. His body is blond, fox-blond. It is tiring to be with him. Whenever Eleanor strays toward sincerity, he smiles very gently behind his hand. He has learned to mimic precisely Eleanor's passionate vowels, dilutes her enthusiasms with sarcasm, drains a conversation of content. This is how he demonstrates his good breeding. In the light of his sometimes brilliant irony, the unruly world grows smaller, small as a pill, in diminishing boxes of parody. He smokes, inhales the smoke luxuriously, fondles and chews the cigarette. He is *resting*, Eleanor decides, he is waiting without impatience. How can he *do* that?

Someone lights the fire at last, behind her, the breath of kindling caught, she looks quick, the edge of skirt gone. It is a good fire, lights the room. Outside, suddenly dark. It doesn't matter.

Then the others arrive all together and it's really night and the house is alive, the lights thrown outside and the snow full of stars. Everybody bundles in, Mary stepping upstairs where she lays her things on Eleanor's pillow, and Eleanor wonders why the hell she has to do things like that, invade like that and touch things where she shouldn't. Mary leaves lipstick on crystal, fingerprints on waxed tabletops, traces of Mary all over the house. Mary kisses everyone, even Eleanor, and for the rest of the evening, Eleanor can smell Mary's perfume on her face, the scent gives her a mild headache. A well-proportioned fire burns in the dining room too. Mary would like a glass of red wine, and Drinkwater pours it for her. Drinkwater has never relished liquor more than since it was prohibited. It is something he and Mary have in common. Not such a bad basis for marriage either; Drinkwater and Mary, forever indulgent, sipping and stroking and snoozing in the sun. DW had better make a lot of money.

Eleanor has a glass or two. Dinner's ready, a little pork roast stuffed with dried prunes and marinated in Madeira. Chutney. Roast potatoes, which are godawful, Christ spring must come, these potatoes are not to be endured. She watches Drinkwater. Sleek as an otter, Drinkwater pulling food from the serving dishes onto his plate, cutting his meat with his fork.

But here is MacDougal sitting beside Eleanor. He is smaller than he seemed that night in January, shorter than Eleanor but then who isn't, short but really perfectly made. And Emma at the head of the table, sipping beef broth critically. She says it's the best she's had since Ottawa, where she had the flu and it was all she could keep down. Emma Partridge, built like one. Definitively buxom, and her beautiful white hair piled on her head in a dishevelled *rouleau*. She is a journalist, a rare bird in these parts. Eleanor doesn't think about it much, but she loves Emma, responds to Emma as if she were a radical creature. Emma says, It's a damn shame the press is making such a ballyhoo out of this socialistic conference down in Calgary because it just makes matters worse all this hide-and-seek in the newspapers, secrecy simply incites the curiosity of the malingering vets, bless their souls, just look at what temperance has done for the booze trade, not to mince words (and a hard look at Mary who is well into the Bordeaux), it's secrecy too, says Emma, makes of sex what it doesn't need to be, all peek-a-boo and how do you do.

DW lights a cigarette before they are quite finished the main course and Mary takes it from him, drags on it and stubs it in her butterplate. Eleanor orders coffee brought in. She isn't prepared for a drunken evening, she needs to listen for MacDougal. She stands and turns the crystal globe at the centre of the chandelier that hangs above the table, dimming the lights. She hears Mary purring in her Chippendale. This is the hour Eleanor loves best, everyone fed, a static, glowy, incandescent evening, a brass pendulum, stopped.

And another thing about MacDougal, his hands are very strange and small, his nails cut square, so clean, and then something that stirs her, his nails, they are polished with a clear polish, she's sure of it, they shine like they're waxed. She crosses her legs. Under the table, her grey cat lisps against her ankles. She has the butler bring port with the coffee, port after all.

The table is cleared. The butler has a graceful way, he sweeps the table with a silver brush, soft as a baby's brush, the bread crumbs and bits of meat fall into a little silver dustpan which he holds beneath the side of the table like a billiard pocket. The tablecloth is a field of snow lit by church spires. Candlelight. The islands of linen, the watery reflections in silverware. Eleanor unbuttons her shoe, slips her foot under her, Emma reaches over, pats her knee, and says, "This young woman has the world by the tail." Drinkwater snorts, catches Eleanor's remote glance, stops himself. Emma goes on to say that she sees a future for women Eleanor's age, and Mary's age too, naturally, now we've won the vote, that's the first small step but why we confused the issue with temperance is beyond me when we've better things to do and anyway it offended the men. MacDougal is quiet, always so quiet damn him, Eleanor feels she must give Emma her eyes, but she's listening for MacDougal, the strange man with the ordinary name, a man with a mouth like that.

Emma says education is the only avenue to power. Up till now it has been a disgrace, women's education, just look at the Agricultural College. (During the war Emma taught agricultural journalism at the Agricultural College; they fired her when the men returned from duty, saying they were short of funds, but Emma maintains she was too modern in her approach.) The poor benighted women in

Home Economics, going to *university* for John's sake, to learn how to look after ten children on a farm? What they *should* be taught is how to *avoid* having one child after another without rest. "There's more interest taken in breeding hogs in Western Canada than there is in breeding children," says Emma. "It's a crime against woman-kind, in the name of modesty." Then she apologizes up and down for doing so much of the talking, but she can't help it, she says, she comes by it honestly, Emma says, she comes from a protesting stock, pioneer and Huguenot blood in her veins, it makes her what she is and she won't back down to anybody.

There follows a familiar discussion about everybody's origins and how many generations everyone has in Canada. Mary says her maternal great-grandfather was twice governor or something of somewhere in Manitoba, and her grandfather was with the Hudson's Bay Company, but the money came from pigs. Eleanor says her grandparents left Scotland in the '30s, and settled on a farm in Ontario. Drinkwater doesn't say. MacDougal says his grandparents left Scotland too, he says, it's obvious from his name, Scotch Gaelic, it means, "son of the dark stranger." Everyone stares at him. MacDougal arranges his knife at a right angle to his dessert fork. So when they're leaving, it's after midnight and the cold can't touch them. Emma kisses Eleanor, both cheeks, like they do in Quebec, and she says, *sub rosa*, "He's got character, my dear, I don't give a fig for the dark stranger, he's from bold stock." She puts her dry hand on Eleanor's long face. "White all through and straight as a string."

We are of the opinion that, in view of the unrest that prevails not only in the Country, but throughout the World, it behoves the T. Eaton Co. as a large Employer of Labour to consider very seriously the question of keeping our staff satisfied and loyal to the Company.

We cannot afford to ignore the fact that Unionism is spreading rapidly amongst our Employees and it is a very militant form of Unionism we have to reckon with today and one that requires very careful handling. We submit that we should endeavour to find a way to narrow the difference between the remuneration received by those in positions of responsibility and the average Worker. If an employee be a married Man, he should live comfortably, keep his family decently and give his children at least a good common-school education. We submit that any Man who works honestly and faithfully during his active years is entitled to be protected against want in old age. Under such conditions, a Man will work more efficiently, loyally and enthusiastically.

The well-known large-heartedness of our President, Sir John, and the kindly consideration for and interest in his Employees, inspires us with confidence that he would welcome any plan that would make for better conditions for the Employees and in any such a way as to cause as little disruption to business as possible. We beg leave to convey the plan enclosed herein, which we feel confident will ensure to the Company greater loyalty on the part of the Employees because they will see in it something better than anything they can expect from Unionism.

Sincerely,
I remain,

Prophets

MACDOUGAL DOESN'T WEAR SLIPPERS; they are soft and too close to the ground. Sitting on the edge of his narrow iron-post bed, MacDougal unfolds last week's News on the ragrug and places his boots there. Good firm boots, and trousers, pressed, a clean white shirt.

It is 10 a.m. His apartment is filled with Boston ferns swaying from wicker baskets, the air is green with the slender sprays of ferns, and African violets. The violets are blooming, beautiful and cautious faces which remind MacDougal of the fine powdered skin of the old women drinking tea at the prayer meetings. The light breaks into prisms through the bevelled glass, MacDougal sits in splashes of spring light, smelling of shaving cream.

Fourteen books lie open on his desk. MacDougal gazes at them in amazement. He worships their shapes, memorizes their titles and authors, he loves the way they begin, full of false promise.

A book is a limpet, a snail, a cuttlefish,
an oyster, the shell of it fascinates
once the inhabitant
has vanished.

But once he gets the drift, once MacDougal gets the gist, his interest flags, the books lie open, dusty in the dry wind. *Forests are burning up north, they say, it's this heat and the drought and the big hot winds from the south. Forests of books are burning.*

Once in a while MacDougal folds the dusty books, his fingers running down the creases of their leather spines, he gathers the wrinkled books in his arms, walks down the narrow wooden stairs to his bookstore, puts the books on his downstairs desk and sits before them, inscribing their names and the names of their publishers and the places and dates of their making, in a tall green ledger with pale blue columns for this purpose. The stacks rise tall as trees, right to the ceiling, and all of them toppling with books, shrouded with dust, classified according to MacDougal's precisely random system. *Repetition* with *Rasselas* (this, a lovely copy, emblems inked in gold, illustrated from etched copper plates coloured with watercolour washes, bound in snake skin), *Men and Women* against *Leaves of Grass*. BOOKS NEW & USED, says MacDougal's storefront, and MacDougal wonders what makes a book *used*. BOOKS ANTI-QUARIAN & OTHERWISE, says the sign on MacDougal's store, and there is a lot of Jack London, and the ceiling is supported by stout pieces of timber around which MacDougal has built more bookcases out of cherry-wood, their shelves fit together without a single nail, and in these bookcases resides the literature that will eventually send him to jail.

But this morning, the Future is amber, it is the future of First Things.

The Bottom Drawer

MacDougal smokes his pipe. He sits at the tin table in his little bedroom. He is so nicely dressed, so crisp. And his room shines like a silver maple, all symmetry, simplicity, and light. He likes tables to be bare, his bed (with its handsewn quilt) is tucked up and empty. It seems he likes a sparse empty place, what poverty might look like if it were dignified. But he clutters his rooms with books and curios. He collects things, keeps them about his rooms to look at, perhaps

46

to touch. Clam shells and stones and a snail shell painted blue, the tiny jaw of a rodent, maybe a squirrel. Wind-up toys, photographs, postcards. He likes photographs of people he doesn't know, close-ups of faces, their eyes directed at the lens. He has so many of these portraits around his place, it looks like he's part of a big community. But he doesn't know them. He keeps his table bare, but a well-polished silver snuff box with the symbol *aleph*, a bear tooth, a beetle shell, a snake skin he once discovered in a rock garden on Trotter's island—he tucks these things into corners where the white curtain sits on the froststained sill. He dusts them with his handkerchief, he puts some of them away in drawers or a jewellery box with plush lining and an absurd pin with Victoria's chubby face upon it.

But his tin table, he keeps empty. Other desks, reading and work benches cluttered with ledgers and notebooks, in the partial light of his affections, books half-finished, abandoned. When he sits at his work places, MacDougal is astonished to discover the notes half-hidden under splayed books, his up-and-down lopped-off handwriting, …*spiritual interpr…n earth of…nd love…* But his tin table is the place for composing the Book, *lowship welc…or race…en free…*like a wave curling back on itself. MacDougal knows he lives at the place where the future meets itself. *y association we…one ano…o nobler tho…higher aspirations, truer li…* These are the days, this is our time.

A Church Sonata

MacDougal has been writing for an hour when the drawstring on his imagination suddenly pulls closed. Anyway, it's time to go. He looks at himself in the single small mirror above the washbasin. He wears dark wool jackets and keeps them clean. He washes and combs his dark hair by touch. He shaves closely in the small mirror. And now it is Sunday morning and he is a guest at the open pulpit at the People's Church. He won't be late. MacDougal sits on his bed to blacken his firm leather boots with a toothbrush.

IDEALIZE THE REAL!
REALIZE THE IDEAL!

His back slouched over his task, MacDougal on a cane chair, his hands toward the window, enjoying the whistle of the brush on the leather, yells suddenly when someone touches his shoulder. Very close beside him is a tall skinny boy with large red ears, staring at MacDougal with bird-eyes. *Brown eyed and innocent,* MacDougal observes, and leans toward him.

"Mum sent me," says the boy. Thin lips, they work the words, buck teeth.

"And who is Mum?" MacDougal's low voice, nearly a whisper.

"My Mum. She's called Anna. At the Mission." Watching MacDougal, he adds, "She's a nurse with you, helping the people that's sick."

"Ahh, yes, Anna Macovitch. Is anything the matter?"

"Yes." Shoves a piece of paper at MacDougal.

MacDougal reads the note. "She's become ill," he says. "Who is looking after you?"

The boy's attention has been drawn to a quilt hung on the wall beside MacDougal's bed. MacDougal looks from him to the quilt. He puts his hand on the boy's shoulder, there's no flesh on him, he'd be a hard child to hold, and he asks him again, "Who is looking after you at home?"

"Oh, there's my aunt and them." His eyes, bird's eyes, make all things equal. "Is Mama going to lose the job, she don't go in tomorrow?"

"No. No, of course not. Tell her it's fine. Tell her we'll manage till she gets well."

The boy is going to leave.

"What's your name?"

"Stevie. Steven like."

"Stevie," says MacDougal. "You would like a, would you want to eat something?"

Stevie shrugs. "No. What's that thing then?"

"That? Yes, well that's a quilt, but I put it on the wall you see because I like to look at it."

The boy lifts his hands in the air, the colours of the quilt are afloat, colour swarming in spring.

MacDougal assumes the teacher's posture and points to the letters sewn on the bright fabric. "Yes, it says 'The Good' here, see? And at the bottom here, 'The Beautiful', and over here, that's 'The True'. And up here?" He stops, remembering his technique, MacDougal the church teacher posing questions. "What's it say here?"

"I don't know." Stevie is patient too.

"You can't read."

"Some."

"Well, up here, it says, 'God.' "

Simple colours and stitchings, pure and untutored. "Listen," he says, sitting again, "why don't you stay while I prepare my sermon? You could draw while you wait. See? I've got a box of chalks."

Stevie perches on the chair and abruptly goes to work while MacDougal reads through his notes, cautiously, afraid his papers will startle this impartial creature.

And Stevie draws a picture. Red house, black chimney, yellow sky, black sun, blue woman lying beside the house, he draws her face, her open mouth, and one yellow eye.

The Canon's Diary

5th April

I miss her tonight. I walked by her closet on some errand, and there she was, or rather there were her clothes hanging, still fragrant with her.

I have felt forsaken, that is the word, forsaken of late. It occurs to me, I am struck dumb at these times. I wish to speak to someone, and find I am beyond speech.

My nightmare has recurred. But last night my hand had been blown off, I don't recall how, but I was wandering through a field, it looked like one at home actually, in fall, after the harrow had been over. But I stumbled over the deep waves in the soil, and I was holding out my arm. My hand had been blown off. I had the taste of blood in my throat. And something else. A man with remarkable eyes, thin they were, they were brown in colour, but he looked sharp, at me. He was the very devil. Dear God, am I to take responsibility for my nightmares too?

Write it out. Room, me in a chair hands tied behind, his face hooded. Hit me hit hit then was hung hands from. A man cannot defend himself, exposed. My stomach was exposed.

Write it out. He skinned me

Willow

DRINKWATER IS NEGLECTING YOUNG MARY. He's always at a meeting these days, why can't he take an evening off once in a while and see her? And Daddy, attending to those strange men with the foreign names. Daddy had been so angry with Reverend Bateman. *A bigot, a cursed bigot, where would he suggest I find labour as reasonable as the Serbs.* But it looks to Mary as though Bateman had been right somehow; the employees at the packing plant *hadn't* shown up for work that morning. But the soldiers had come round and they'd climbed up onto the loading dock, Daddy said, and nearly scared him to death. So he'd promised then and there to let the foreigners go and replace them with vets.

But he never did. And now he's always meeting somebody and Mother's upstairs too sick to come down.

Mary wanders. She eats a half box of cherries. She stares out the window at the April light, the perfect images in melted snow, the scarcity of elms. She walks very slowly up the stairs. It's nearly impossible to lift her feet, she drags them and has to sit a minute on the top stair.

The sick room, dark, she opens the window, then turns toward the bed. Her mother seldom wakens now. The bruises around her eyes are deep and wide. Mary sits on the edge of the bed, listens for the breathing, watching for the movement of the blankets. She places her hand against the face and runs her thumb beside the mouth. There, that is the small bundle of muscle that pulls your mouth sideways in your lopsided smile, there, the knuckle of flesh that would, there, touch it, dimple in.

The geese are returning early this year and it hasn't been a warm spring. Mary has taken her mother's shawl and gone out through the French doors that open onto the small terrace that sits above the solarium. Summers, as a child, Mary would sleep out here on the chaise, and her mother would stay with her.

> *husha, you are sleeping*
> *my hands on*
> *you my magic*
> *lantern*

Together they would sleep here, summer nights. There are snow geese too. Mary hears the silver anguish in their voices. The doors are open. It's cold. Across the yard, broken willows, the frozen river, wide, the ice shifting, the echo of whales. She looks back to the open door in a shudder of wind. The geese fly north. Mama Mama, they cry.

Reservoirs

HE IS DRIVING IN THE WRONG DIRECTION. He knows it. It's nearly three and he hasn't been back to the office since lunch. He should be going north, to work, things can't wait. So he doesn't know what will happen from one minute to the next, the road rising up and falling a few feet behind him, like he is treading a small globe.

Maybe it's this sunshine today, got him restless, uneasy. If he could just go play golf, that would be one thing, but it's still too early, there's snow yet, see it in the bushes, in the ditches full of blue ice. But it's the first day the sun has carried any warmth, and it really is hot, sunshine and gravel dust and the roof up yet on his roadster forms a vacuum. Finally, he must stop to get some air and decide where he's going, because he's miles from anywhere now, nearly in La Salle, by the snow-swollen river risen up to the banks, Drinkwater stopping his car at last in the middle of the wooden bridge.

He sees the fox before he recognizes it as Fox, a rare event, a sighting, not yellow or red but long and her (for Drinkwater says "her" in his mouth, his lips closed on his moist cigarette), and her shoulders—this stays with Drinkwater for the rest of his life, how the she-fox's shoulders slouch—she is slouching by the culvert choked by debris and spring run-off, skirting the grass growing now a little in the snow, she runs in front of him, daring? insolent? She is in the woods on the other side, a piece of light in the woods, gone. He memorizes her after she has gone. He drops his cigarette still long, a thing he likes to do, to waste his wasteful cigarette.

The air blows chilly from the river. He lights another cigarette, reluctant to blow out the match. Leaning against the railing, his hands crossed, smoking. This wasn't the bridge but it was at this time of year nearly to the day. He was 12 and he doesn't remember the date, but he knows it happened on a Wednesday because he had a stupid piano lesson. He had been sleepy and putting in time, trying hard to ignore the moronic persuasions of Mrs Little the piano instructor when he heard his mother cry out.

His father had been a bridge builder and he had been one of the innovators, dredging reservoirs and dams. He'd been successful and they were left with a lot of money. His father had been an early success, making his fortune in his early 20s, building dams and bridges. He was 42 when he jumped off.

And every day since that Wednesday has been a square mile between Drinkwater and his father's suicide. He has collected the days like he collects real estate and investments. His acquisitions are the space between him and his father's black passion. But the river breaking beneath him tells him otherwise. Today is Wednesday. And money is made of paper.

Drinkwater has the will-power of a reformed alcoholic. He drops the cigarette into the water, and walks to his car. Very carefully, he backs up, and turns it around on the mud road, heading back to town.

April

A PALE FRECKLED PRESBYTERIAN puts his old lips, moist as mould, against
Eleanor's cheek and says, "Never mind lassie, the snow will soon
go." He covers Eleanor's hand with his, a red-headed man gone grey,
liver-flecked. "Cold hands! And a warm heart to match," he says.
The hand returns to her cheek, squeezes her face between the
cheekbone and jaw. He has dribbled dainties down his brown silk
vest. Dream Biscuits.

She slips past him, outside. It snowed again last night. Eleanor
is glad. She wraps herself in her brown velvet coat, sticks her chin
in her collar, the ground gives under step, gives way nothing like
winter at all. Winter was all resistance. This soft ground, the
movement of sparrows over the brindled cemetery—Eleanor grieves
over the lost winter, the still and solemn season of waiting for her
aunt's death. Waiting is over.

The aunts and sisters-in-law who organized the funeral have
been harping at the florists all week long. Finally the grocer of all
people said *he* could get them daffodils, lord knows how, but then
his brother in B.C. got sick or something and they had to settle for
poinsettias. They are white poinsettias. Eleanor is glad it snowed last
night. The afternoon light is the colour of onionskin.

Why are they burying her over here? It's miles from any other grave. She must be expecting company. It's a big crowd for a woman's funeral, even made the morning paper—some of the aunts consider this unseemly. Apparently ladies die in camera. Eleanor is one of the first in the parade of mourners and when she stops, so do many of the others. The mourners form their semi-circle at least 20 feet from the grave, some of them breaking away to form an uneven inner circle. But the effect is straggled, people stand sideways to the grave, the Canon turns his back to it, staring despondently into the muffled trees.

Out of some bizarre sense of propriety, the young children are led to the very brink. They stare into the snow-flecked hole with blank faces, twist cold toes in peppery mud. The drizzled coffin, the dizzy snow.

Auntie Lizzbeth'd been the best Auntie ear nibbler, she made up singsongs and never forgot a funny joke. That's her, in that wood box, in that muck. And that's a sore wind still blowing even though it's sposed to be April.

Eleanor's parents are standing, absorbed, outside the ragged circle. Their faces empty, they hold hands, expect no comfort. They don't look for Eleanor, don't wonder where she is.

But Mary is in motion. Eleanor sees her narrow face. Mary is turned sideways and she looks back at the grave wall-eyed, supported on either side by Drinkwater and some other fellow, Walter. The three of them are wavy on the sodden ground. *Damn it, Mary's sorrowing. Whose bones does she pity?*

Eleanor, walking toward them, they are far from her and she must walk a long ways to reach them. She has the feeling they are all in separate lifeboats on the sea, separated by great slow waves. She must be standing beside her young cousin now, she is towering over her, Mary looking up at her. See the terror in Mary's blue eyes.

And beneath us, nothing. We are floating on the surface. Mary's face is falling from her bones, her face like crumpled paper. We are fictions. Time, dust, haphazard increments, on our faces, in our empty arms. Our empty hands caress each other, ruffle the surface of the sea.

"Eleanor, be an angel and take these upstairs to the men."

Glad to, get me out of this hive, Christ this tray's heavy though.
Eleanor kicks at the door at the top of the staircase. She enters the billiard room, her favourite, great high ceiling, sash windows, Eleanor can see more fat snow. A fire pops, the click of billiard balls, the company of Men. The Canon is here. Eleanor is fond of this baffled old man. He takes the tray from her and tries gallantly to set it on the sideboard, spills the cream, Eleanor glances from the splash of cream on silver into his papery face, and they smile into each other. Old friends.

Drinkwater is talking about the Metal something, a council, Eleanor doesn't know if it's workers or owners. She can't hear well. The Board of Trade, contracts and councils, the Norris government, the Banks. Words wash over Eleanor, she tries to net them and they fin through her fingers. She sits beside the Canon. He absently takes her hand and doesn't let go, playing with her single ring, patting her hand till her skin chafes. Eleanor and the Canon follow the darting conversation of the gentlemen like two old cats hungering after goldfish. Here and there, phrases stipple the surface, submerge, disappear.

The Canon's Diary

April 15

Been well. Weather permitting my daily walk. I have felt well for days past. Perhaps the dreams are over. Time heals all.

It was like walking back from null. But this morning I feel almost a child, picking pussywillow with Rachael, oh we were happy, I can honestly say, when we were young. And when I think of the poor children growing up caged by the city, when we had the entire prairie for our play. How old I have grown. How strange.

War.

Such a little word. Much in nothing where we all met. We met in the war, where we were. It is Terror, to be known, in this,

Enough is enough. I remember my mother, she wore my father's clothes to work outside, mending the yard after winter. She was a beautiful woman. I remember her fine bones and the look of her honest blue eyes. She had wonderful health. The look of her breathing deeply with such satisfaction in the return of spring. Gather the pussywillows, gather.

I will be well. They are meeting with the iron masters next week. They will need support, if an old man has anything to give. Oh buck up Albert. I'm getting soft.

Walter is a Worried Man

WALTER HAS BEEN with the Sir Rodney Trotter family since 1906. He is their chauffeur, and their gardener, and their boatman. Sir Rodney likes to think that he has "taken the boy in." Walter left them, to serve overseas for three years. Now he's back. Things have changed.

she traces
the dozing
buds on the bushes

He came back, to his rooms above the converted stable. They're the fanciest rooms he's ever had. Before the war, this luxury and Walter's exclusive place in it had seemed like a natural thing. The Sir Rodney Trotters had too much; Walter had nothing; Walter would live upon their excess, not like a parasite, but like a product of plenty, some kind of fruit growing, fertile.

she
studies
the first
tickle of spring

He came back, and the rooms are still the fanciest he's ever had, and Sir Rodney still treats him with elaborate deference, persistently astonished at Walter's mechanical abilities, skirting any discussion of the war with reverential silence.

she listens
to its
hesitations

Walter came back, to the lacy curtains and the soft bed and the room that is all his. But he wonders, why does he feel murderous toward these pretty things? He has come back, like the perpetual third person. But his homecoming, to the lustre, the thick-painted beauty and sunlight of the place, has been a collision, a catastrophe.

its mewings and
gurgles,
the early
voices of May.

He walks through the peace, wealth, and finery, and there is still trench mud on his boots, he is reeking of chloride of lime, of the dead too dead for naming.

A Slender Young Thing

Walter has known Mary since she was seven years old. She was a friend of his, in her own perverse way. She bit him and pinched him and stole from him. She understood that nothing would ever be reported back to her parents. This was a little war entirely between themselves. And on the rare occasions when Walter pinched her back, she accepted the tear-stinging pain like a trooper and never told a soul. And when he left to go to war, she lay under his bed while he packed. And when he had offered to kiss her goodbye, she had pretended to whisper one final secret and then nearly bit off the soft lobe of his ear. She was always one for putting strange things in her mouth.

But Mary has changed. Walter has never seen her *humble*. Since early April, since the funeral, Mary has been fairly human. Walter has watched her roam the grounds, looking thoughtful, almost compassionate. Walter has never seen young Mary consider the possibility of life outside her fine-tuned senses. He has been watching her closely, looking into those relentless blue eyes, searching hopelessly for the familiar signs of cynicism and malice. But something has happened to Mary. His Nasty-Mary was somebody you could cheerfully despise. Now she simpers, now she tries to please. Mary has become "womanly," a *slender young thing.* Too soon, someone will love her and before anyone knows it, she'll be Happy, an angel in a three-storey Adamesque house in Crescentwood. Walter is very restless as he goes to work, introducing tender young poison ivy plants to the shrubbery around Crescentwood Park across the street.

Mary, 21 years old, and feeling every inch a slender young thing, is performing a function quite new to her. She is *thinking.*

Of course, she has thought before. But this is different from the kind of thinking that gets you from one spot to the next or puts chocolates in your mouth. There's a new voice in Mary's nimble mind. A sort of echo. It's dazzling. Especially since Mama's death, Mary has been listening for this new reverberation, and practising with it like a new-found instrument. Adroit, she is learning to carry on an outward conversation, with DW, or her father, or poor Walter, and at the same time have this other voice, a contradiction, a joke. It makes the green lawn roll out a little further, it patterns the blue sky like hand-painted wallpaper, over and over and over. She stretches in it. The world is like a bath.

Mary is still not convinced thinking is any different from feeling, rubbing up against things. The good thing about thinking, Mary thinks, is you can rub up against really unpleasant things without actually hurting yourself. Mary never wears anything but pure gold or maybe sometimes pure silver; alloys give her a rash. Mary never wears rough wool next to her skin; not exactly a rash, but it's just not nice, against your skin like that. Mary has never thought any kind of thought that might hurt her in real life. It would be stupid,

Mary thinks, to let your own mind hurt you. A different kind of vanity, if you really think about it.

Mary sits on the bench beside the duck pond and admires her small feet resting dainty in greening grass. She studies her fingernails, spots a stray hair on the front of her dress. Suddenly she strains forward, nearly getting wet, lets a deep frown tuck between her pretty eyes, almost careless, and she says, thinking Walter's still puttering in the roses behind her, "Walter, lazy man, is that really a crayfish in my pond? Are they edible?"

Walter has just finished his errand and is walking casually back across Harvard. He's 6'4", and still skinny. He thinks he'll let the patrician think she's having him drive her to the Hudson's Bay store and he'll just slip into the Labour Temple a minute, let her wait in the car.

Mary, sitting artfully on the grass beside the pond when he returns, stabs at the crayfish with the poker which she has taken from Walter's own fireplace. "Where were you?" she says. "You exasperate me Walter. Do you know these shy pink creatures have proliferated in my pond since you've been gone?"

"Yeah," says Walter, "there are more of them."

"How do they do it, Walter?"

"They dream each other Mary, you know that."

"Take me shopping Walter, let's go right now, I want to."

"Well if that's the case, I'll fetch the Packard like a good man."

"Right," says Mary. She's still looking into the pond, pulls up her sleeve and reaches into the scummy water, plucks a snail from a lily pad—another transplant of Walter's from the island at Lake of the Woods. "Would these skimpy things ever get big enough to eat? Like those parsley ones we had in Paris before the stupid war."

But Walter has gone like a good man, and Mary, alone, sniffs at the snail, and quick, holds the black leechy body to her tongue. Hmmmm, muddy fishy.

The Boys of the Old Red Patch

Walter drives Mary downtown. Mary is afraid of the car, though she loves to be seen in it, loves to be seen in anything splashy and nice. The aqua-blue Packard should be just the thing for a joy-ride, and Mary works very hard to actually feel as blasé as she looks, but the thing is, she's squirrely, her nerves can't take it, they gnaw, they curl like burnt paper. Mary's only experience with physical pain comes in this form, the startled nerves clawing up her back, though she sits, extract of insouciance, dressed up like Wedgewood, perfectly coordinated.

It is worse downtown. Mary has many private fears, most of them subverted by her ready petulance. Except for Machinery. The mechanical is Mary's nightmare: motor-cars, trolleys, even the new electric washing machines. Mary yearns for the good old days, when the maids squeezed the laundry through the double-wringer, sweating quietly, the comforting rhythm, soft rain water dripping from scrubbed lace.

Walter tips his cap at a man at the corner of Broadway and Balmoral—goggly man, looks like he wears a suit in the morning and takes it off piece by piece all day, shirt sleeves rolled up now, collar off, jacket over his arm, funny thick lips this man, face too something, Mary decides, too smart or something. "Who's that?" she asks Walter. "Someone you met in the army?"

"Someone I met last week. Works at the Metal Trades Council, met him through your friend, little who-who the house builder, the pup, what's his name, Drinkwater."

"Drinkwater is not a pup. You're an insolent old man Walter." She looks back at the Metals man. "DW knows him? Why?"

Walter smiles, says, "Drinkwater doesn't know him very well. He should. And he will. Won't be long now."

"Won't be long till I'm car sick," says Mary.

Walter pulls in front of Market Square. Mary climbs down, and strays to a bench in Victoria Park. Walter sits beside her, looks at her lime face and shoves her bobbed little head between her knees. She's too desperate to complain, and Walter marvels at her unexpected compliance. He forgets she's in this posture, forgets his own hand heavy on her head, he sits in wonder while a giant man crosses King Street, climbs the speakers' box, removes his shirt, draws ropes from his baggy pants, ties them about his huge chest. A crowd gathers. Walter removes his hand from Mary's head, she sits up, forehead swollen with blood. Walter drags Mary up to the stage, using her as an excuse to push to the front, a poor excuse apparently, someone pokes his ribs. Walter is mesmerized and Mary is delighted with this tremendous creature, wearing some kind of loin-cloth now, bound with ropes, staring at the crowd, smiling a little, confident. His muscles look to Mary like loaves of bread, but they must be hard, resistant. He's got a jaw like a hammer, anticipating. Suddenly he lifts his arms, pectoral, biceps, rectus abdominus, turns half-circle, deltoid, triceps, gluteus maximus, all bound with these ropes, the man takes a deep breath, shouts, the ropes break and fly off, the big one from his chest hits Mary on her neck, not too hard, pops a pearl button. Walter doesn't even notice, selfish dope. The crowd's laughing with relief, and sporting Mary laughs too. The muscled jaw moves, he speaks! "At Whippers, I saw many people die." Mary looks in alarm at Walter. Walter whispers, "Ypres."

"Many young men, friends of mine, massacred for a few acres of foreign soil."

"Let's go," Mary tugs at Walter. "Let's go!"

"One day, when the fighting was over for a while, I sat in a shelled-out garden, and watched another of my friends, a Highlander, bleed to death, his boots full of blood. He was 21."

"Sssick!"

"We didn't bury him and we didn't grieve. We went on fighting. And today, I know why."

Mary pinches Walter's arm, whispers, "Is this going to be another one of your bleating workers? Because if it is, I'm going shopping."

Walter doesn't take his eyes off the muscleman, bends his lips to Mary's ear, says, "Leave now, you're walking."

"I hate you," says Mary.

"I'm only grateful that we didn't look back, that we didn't wander from our purpose, which was simply to win the war. Because if we'd wondered about it, we all might have died."

"I've *seen* him somewhere, he was wearing clothes. I don't trust you, Walter, you're not a trustworthy man."

"And the only thing I carry with me from that bloody confusion is the comradeship with my fellow soldiers, my fellow slaves of the master class."

"It *is* another bleating socialist! Damn you Walter!"

Mary marches to the car. Well, the only thing to do now is to *buy* that grey silk. I'm so mad, I could bite him!

Fire

YOU WANT TO KNOW what I think? You asking me? Everybody here, every single son of a bitch here, got a place in the sun. Brotherhood. Tell me about it. I got Brothers lining up night after night and every one of them putting a dollar in the collection box, right? Brotherhood.

I go to church. Me and my friend Aileen. She says, Come on Bonnie we're going to the new church. So I go.

It ain't no new church, not to me it ain't. Most ways, it's worse, like they tossed some more coal on the old fire, it burns hotter, but me it still leaves cold. Like they'd tie me up and toast me for kindling, their righteous old fire.

But the funny thing about this, me and Aileen are sitting proper and the minister or whatchacallim kind of saying the world's gonna go up in smoke and some kind of new one come and I wanna laugh cause every word he's saying I could whisper to some john in bed and it'd finish the job quick as a dime.

Confession

THE HAND LOTION IS THE COLOUR of pearls, and it has a pink label that says it is made of finely powdered pearls ground thin as ash under glass and then mixed with oils aromatic and something called lanolin made of lambs' wool creamy and fat. Eleanor drops lanolin and pearls in her broad palms, soothes the pink knuckles like smiles, the pale moons at the tips of her long dry fingers.

Outside, and she knows this because the Men are removing the storm windows today and the windows are opened for the first time since October and little breezes are chilly but it is so wonderful to feel them moving and living, outside there is a flat-sounding bird, it squeezes in and out comes this squeaking song or a bicycle wheel squealing, brrrippp, brrrippp, and if she listens closely the trains are moaning low as underground, they bang low as lead somewhere far off downtown. Nestling bushes pucker with new leaves.

It is easy to wear a dark blue dress when it's cotton with small roses and yellow lace, easy to brush and braid brown hair, tuck it with a ribbon, comb it with tortoiseshell. And her complexion in spring morning air is calm, calm. Only listen. And there is the stir of MacDougal's horses. Eleanor watches MacDougal descend from the carriage and give the horses over to one of the Men. Graceful and precise, MacDougal moves through the washed morning air, fine as crystal and changing in the light. She runs down to meet him at the door.

They are shy just now, pleasantly so. MacDougal follows her to the sunroom that's sunnier than summer when the Virginia creeper is in leaf. But whereas tapestries, a desk with pigeon-holes for papers thin with the necessities of a big business, paintings and vases above and upon a grand piano, whereas all these things once gave Eleanor a *name*, the secure feet-on-the-ground knowledge of herself as *Eleanor*, daughter of, sister of, niece of, cousin of, member of—but owner of nothing, not really, it all belongs to Father, to her remaining brother who is running the firm in Toronto, to her uncles and their sons, and she doesn't know how to run the house and she hates the Country Club and the Yacht Club and the Hunt Club because she doesn't know how to golf or sail and she's afraid of horses. She wonders why MacDougal would come to see her today. He probably feels sorry for her.

So the room becomes foolish and flimsy when MacDougal follows Eleanor to the couch. He has been to the Mission, he says, it is going very well yes thank you (he is really grateful for her interest? yes he is, always genuine). What exactly do you do there? she asks and she is thinking, well the hell with it he knows I'm an idiot and I might as well find out, what goes on there, at the Mission? she asks. MacDougal isn't even sarcastic with her, he doesn't seem to expect her to know anything, why should he expect anything, when he knows she runs on a short leash in this goddam suffocating city. He tells her there's a kindergarten and a library, a gymnasium and a kitchen, a chapel and the Reverend's office, Eleanor should go see it sometime, there's a swimming-pool in the basement, of all things. A swimming-pool in the basement! Yes! And Eleanor and MacDougal laugh, he slides down on his chair, so at home with himself, his voice has remarkable range, low to high, large to small, his wonderful voice goes gentle as he explains that there is a swimming-pool in the basement of the Mission, Eleanor should go there soon, she could hear the children's voices echo laughter and splashing (so, to explain the children's splashing laughter, MacDougal takes the mother-of-pearl dish from the sidetable and he holds the shell to his ear, listens, eager).

But Eleanor wants to know, what was MacDougal doing there today? She asks him this, but her own voice is getting long, the words are slow to start and then flip like fish out of a net, splattering and stuttering, oh god. The vowels nearly endless sit fragile and empty as cups on the consonants that are breathy and soggy with the spilled o's and u's and sometimes y's. She doesn't know how to sit either and she wishes from the bottom of her vacant soul she really would care for the Mission as Mission and nothing for herself. But what was MacDougal doing at the Mission so early today?

Today at the Mission, we held classes for the immigrants. What did we teach them? Nothing. These people, mostly from the Ukraine, might speak three languages but none of them are English. Today we had a class in the management of finances, you might say, at least they learned the words for purchasing food. We intended to teach them some of the words for the bank, opening accounts, arranging loans. They haven't much use for banking though. It was a budgetary meeting for people with no money.

But there it is again, just as MacDougal says "money" there's the bell and clatter of a bicycle, surely it's here at Eleanor's front door. Eleanor chooses this moment to tell something to MacDougal, mesmerized as she is, she's afraid to take her eyes from his face, to listen, *will someone answer the bloody door?* why she would choose this moment to tell MacDougal—but what *will* she tell MacDougal? *No one will answer the door*, the bell is ringing, Eleanor is positive she hasn't taken her eyes from MacDougal's face, but he says, gently, "You'd better answer it yourself." So, dizzy with the excesses of confession, *but what will she confess?* Eleanor rustles to the front door which is open and she catches the quick dart of a messenger boy, his small muddy shoes pedalling, the unvoiced breath of a boy pedalling hard over the kentuckythick lawn.

May 1st

The note has been dropped on the floor of the vestibule, an envelope with MacDougal's full name written on it. How the hell did anyone know he was here? I can't even get a letter and it's my own goddam house. Eleanor, tightening the leash on her erratic self-esteem, steers herself casually through the dark drawing-room. *I'm a boat, a scow with a torn sail, popping and prodding through whitecaps from behind the breakwater.* Back to MacDougal who is sitting down again on the other side of the room to be out of the hot sun. After the sharp sunlight, Eleanor can't see MacDougal clearly, he is a fine small figure in the checkered shadow. She holds the letter vaguely in his direction, feels him take it. He's neither surprised nor blown-up about receiving it, runs his thumb inside to open it. Eleanor won't look, would be like Mary wouldn't it to peek, but before she averts her long face, Eleanor sees it's a typewritten letter but that's all, she won't look further, it's not any of my business.

But after MacDougal has left the house (after the not-fond but entirely distracted farewell), Eleanor does pick up the letter, because there has never been any reason in her entire life to obey those silent restraints.

Remember Mary's father, when even the parents must have been young, and Mary's father had said the blessing and as he sliced into one of his own Wiltshire hams, thick slices of pink meat, the generous ham with bubbles of honeyed fat, this sanguine, tongue-coloured man with the silver goatee, the rimless glasses, a face yearning for the years to endorse its own solemnity, Mary's father, saying, Children there is one rule I have followed always to the best of my modest ability and that is to keep to the ways of the Lord in my private moments much as I keep to His ways in my public life.

Fine for you with a life that is public with your Methodist Church, your Conservative Party, your Estate. As for me in my house, I will learn what I can. She reads the letter. Everything conspires to exclude Eleanor from any intimate understanding of the events disclosed: the serif typeface, the toothpick of a signature standing on an official position with a formal organization—The Labour Church. The *Labour* church?

Church: Black velvet hats on stout women, the minister preaching the virtues of hard work, The Lord giveth and the Lord taketh away, but He mostly giveth.

Labour: got used to inflationary wages during the war and now they won't settle down and accept the discipline commensurate with sacrifice, for the sake of the Nation.

Labour: you don't do it on a Sunday.

Labour Church: spontaneous combustion.

At the top of the letter is a seal, a clumsy sketch of an open Bible inside a ring on which is written, *If any man will not work, he shall not eat.* Well, I'm not a man and I don't work, but I wish and I wonder, *Let me in!*

Pigs

DRINKWATER'S MADDER THAN he's ever been before. It's bloody hot, he hasn't had time to bathe, and it's been an absolutely punishing day, one committee meeting after another and nobody willing to listen to reason. Well at least he might have a minute to talk things over with Mary's dad tonight, he needs some relief he does, wish to hell I were out on the links right now I've had it up to here with this imbecile stupidity and now they've gone and voted for a strike when all they needed to do was negotiate like gentlemen one at a time but no they've got to go all out in a mass makes you want to puke not a real gentleman among them not even anything you'd call a craftsman nothing but rabblerousers and bolshevists. And here are the Banks on one hand willing to keep the prices high to avoid declining markets and how's a man expected to stay on top of things with them joining up in secret behind our backs lousy bunch of foreigners. No use saying anything to Mary either, only bore her or what's worse she'd have an O-pinion about it.

So Mary and Drinkwater sit quietly in the garden waiting for dinner to be announced. Mary watches DW even while she concentrates on her book. A cat slides out from the spindly shade provided by snowburnt cedars to deposit the tiny rump of a squirrel under Mary's chair.

Shall we dine?

She lays her book upon the blue cushion, sees her calico's dappled coat, stoops to touch. The cat crouches over his meal. Mary studies the cat's wild dinner, carefully, memorizing, nothing will spoil this evening, it is just a question of self-control.

Nothing will spoil Mary's evening because tonight she and Drinkwater will announce their engagement and it will be a silk cape of a night, it will wrap Mary up in its dignity and its elegance and forever after life will be a calm ocean crossed in the luxuryliner of joint fortunes and Drinkwater will carry a walkingstick and he will place one hand in the pocket of his evening coat, just so.

A Methodist Millionaire

Mary's father is left-handed. Every evening that Sir Rodney is free to spend in the comforts of home, the kitchen-maid places the roast on the table before him with the carving knife arranged on the *right* side of the platter, and that side of the pork, lamb, beef or fowl which offers the best advantage to the carver toward his *right* hand, and every evening Rodney turns the heavy plate around to the left without spilling a single teaspoon of the juices, and without uttering a single syllable of protest. Sir Rodney came from a hard-working Methodist family and he'll not forget his origins.

> *Not more than others have we deserved*
> *but thou hast given us more.*

Some of the older employees at Sir Rodney Trotter's meat processing plant can recall the early days when Rodney would sleep on a park bench near the train station in one of the little towns on his tours rather than pay for a night's lodging for what would amount, after all, to only a few hours' sleep. Rodney has covered the entire grain belt, cajoling farmers to switch from the 300-pound ball-of-lard Berkshire, to the longer leaner Yorkshires. And Sir Rodney's success can be attributed to his own hard work and the perspicacity of like-minded breeders who see the advantage of lighter leaner cleaner hogs altogether different from their corpulent American neighbour got fat by eating the corn in the cattle turds. Because Rodney is a man with an ear to the Future, and even as a young man just set out to earn his way, Rodney could hear the wingthrumming of change. Back in the '90s when a workingman spent himself against the land without so much help from machinery, you could sell bacon with five or six inches of fat on it, all the lean cut away and sold for fresh. But now, a labouring man just doesn't need so much fuel, and he wouldn't thank you for larded bacon like that, even if you gave it to him.

Know Your Bacon!

Because the truth is, Rodney made a killing during the war. He just couldn't help making more and more money. Denmark was selling most of its bacon to Germany, and the English and Irish couldn't feed their own population much less feed the army too. Britain needed huge quantities of Canadian bacon, and Rodney was the man to get it to them, even if he had to go to Chicago and buy it out from under the noses of the Americans. Sir Rodney Trotter's exports of hog products ran at $2 million in the last peacetime year, and ballooned to $4 million in 1915. The new buyer was the War Office, and they bought up all they could get of Trotter's bully beef too. He was a bullet. Profits shot up from $125,000 in 1914, to $480,000 by March 1915. The War was a terrible tragedy, lord knows. But it was a great boon for business.

Entre Nous

Mary is right. Nothing does spoil a lovely evening. Daddy is perfect, as usual, so long as he's coddled a bit. He's an old dear he really is. Mary's always afraid to let her eyes wander from his while they are together like this at the dinner table. It has become almost unbearable since Mother died; now Mary is the only one who can invent the world according to Sir Rodney's peculiar vision. Some people must be protected from themselves.

She lets the men have their cozy time together, gives them a feeling of independence. Off they go, puffing and sonorous, to Rodney's study. "A day of mixed weather. Blessings," says Rodney, bending to kiss Mary's forehead as he passes her chair, "and affliction." Taking the arm of his future son-in-law, guides young Drinkwater to his dark sanctuary, a rare privilege.

DW stands. He's nervous. He'd like a drink but Rodney's a teetotaller. Drinkwater will go out after this is all over and find a friend to share a drink. On a night like this, DW knows, he could drink a whole bottle of brandy and it wouldn't touch him, he's that stirred up.

Now Rodney, on the other hand, never gets excited. Look at him, sitting at his big desk out of habit, rummaging through the bottom drawer like he's forgotten I'm here. Finally, Rodney takes a small wooden box from the drawer and removes from it a fairsized piece of rock or something which he hands mysteriously to DW. It's so rough to touch DW instantly wants to return it, prevents that instinct, studies it closely. Its irregular shape disturbs Drinkwater, its protuberances, and the diversity of its components. It's damn ugly. He looks helplessly at Rodney.

"Guess what it is," says Rodney, who is pleased to have the patience for a game, a rare event.

"It's a rock I guess."

"Ahhh, but look closely boy," says Rodney, and he relieves Drinkwater of the piece, focussing a magnifying glass upon it. "Limestone. Picked it up in Alberta years ago. Just look at the fossils melded into one solid mass. What does it tell you?"

It doesn't tell Drinkwater a damn thing, but he knows Rodney well enough to trust that this flight of fancy will touch down within a minute or two. So he smiles, and through the smallest exertion of will, his eyes warm against Sir Rodney's. Conspirators.

"You're about to tell me about my own mortality sir."

Rodney has a really strange laugh, an intaken breath, like dusty brakes, followed by a wheezy burst of air.

"NNNgggg Paaahaha."

Rodney is holding the limestone in his two white hands. His face reorganized, he says, "I'm sorry to hear about your labour difficulties son. It's a trial, but I'm sure we can overcome these afflictions."

Drinkwater hasn't given much thought to overcoming his trouble with the unions. It has been his plan to take some time off this summer, get married and all that, and wait till his craftsmen are ready to come back to work. But he does like the sound of the Royal *We.* Rodney is famous for his handling of labour difficulties. Drinkwater couldn't find a more ingenious mentor.

Rodney's method is to appeal to the higher feelings of his employees, their loyalty to a company which has, after all, advanced their wages when business has been good, and without waiting for any demands from organized labour. At times when other manufacturers have been reducing the wages of their employees, if Trotter's Meats is bullish, the wages go up. But in exchange, Rodney must demand, and this is only fair any man can see that, that the workpeople accept his frank statement that business is not now in a condition to warrant any advance, in fact, due to stringent conditions of business it is now necessary to call on our employees for a full day's work on Saturday without any extra pay.

Rodney is a sanctimonious butcher. Drinkwater respects that. He envies Rodney. I'd never get away with that kind of talk now. I guess I was born at the wrong time.

But Rodney is concentrating on his piece of limestone, though he's tired by now of his own analogy, another one of the rhetorical blunders Rodney feels it his duty to make. The trouble is, you must come such a long way from the particular to the general. There is the limestone, on first glance an unremarkable bit of greyish rock, but look closely and see the infinite particularities of individual lives which would by themselves be lost to dust, through melding and fusion, the one become a whole, stronger than time, in fact, welded in the heat and pressure of time. He is quiet for so long, staring at the piece of rock, Drinkwater wonders if he has forgotten what he was going to say. This is a baffling thing about the old man: he's such a tough sonofabitch in business, yet on the personal side, you want to make sure he's ok.

"I could use some advice on this labour question," says Drinkwater, prompting.

There's real perplexity and pain in Rodney's face when he looks quickly at DW, it scares the bejeezus out of him, his throat is begging for a brandy.

"I must be getting old," says Rodney.

"Oh no sir," says DW and puts a hand on his arm.

Rodney shrugs his narrow shoulders. He knows this is true but it really doesn't matter, *there will be a greater reward.* "The world is becoming a foreign place for men like me," Rodney says. "And when I hear myself saying such things I know it is true. I am getting old."

"You're still a young man yet. And maybe next year, there will be a grandchild," says Drinkwater, *Jeezus what am I saying here, it's like there's a script I have to follow.*

Rodney is relieved that the moment has passed when he has to figure out the limestone parable. His hands find wonderful relief too in the lighting of his pipe. "It's a question of the individual taking precedence over the community." And Drinkwater is enormously relieved, the old man is himself once again, and this endless night is nearly over. "These disturbances only serve to magnify the differences between classes. Fragments of the community organized wholly for their own benefit. Then, once they gain power, they want to dictate what is right for the rest of us. And they frighten the politicians into going along with it. It's not my wish to frighten you, son, but we're in grave danger."

We're Going to Hell in a Handbasket

All workers, including the Building Trades' Council, went on strike on Thursday morning, May 1st, after holding in the convention hall of the Industrial Bureau, the greatest meeting in the history of the Building Trades' Council. 1,199 Yes. 74 No. NO MORE DEFEAT!

Western Labour News

It's so late, it's almost early. Drinkwater drives out to his building site. He's all hopped up on apricot brandy, been drinking with Bill Popp since he left Mary's house after dinner. It's cool at last, but the day's heat and a night of sticky booze still cling to DW like the memory of some exaggerated passion. He must be tired. Usually a nightdrive like this can make him feel like he can really think, like he can remember every nickel, every nibble, the words to every song he ever heard. But he seems to be following a cold scent, out to the edge of Crescentwood where he has three new starts. He must be doing 45 miles an hour, but he can't even scare himself into focus.

He rolls to the edge of his new development, can see the pale frames, the mountains of brick. The road is mud-rutted. He pulls up under a gabled roof. There are no candles burning in the watchman's hut. His crew abandoned him yesterday after the strike vote.

When Drinkwater looks at the wood frames, he sees a finished house, expensive, brick covered with Virginia creeper, unabashed imitations, Tudor, Dutch colonial, Georgian. He sees the verandah on the side, a bit of stained glass in the transom, fan-shaped, a Mansard roof with eyebrow dormers. The dry rubble becomes a smooth lawn with topiary shrubs, a wrought iron fence, tall and spiked, with Tyndall stone columns at the driveway, what the hell, lots of Tyndall stone, DW sees a rusticated Tyndall stone base, and a Tyndall stone sidewalk. DW, sticking to the leather upholstery of his roadster, sipping brandy from a silver flask, looks into the stark early spring night and he sees *the future*.

MAYOR SEEKS TO AVERT GENERAL STRIKE!
Radical Change or Revolution is Predicted

MacDougal enjoys insomnia. He likes the way it makes the words explode in his mouth, like pop-corn, words and memories surfacing like fish bubbles in a dark lake. Insomnia is MacDougal's vice, the one he nourishes. The empty streets, the polka-rhythms of the barking dog, MacDougal walking beside budding shrubs, through quiet residential streets; they appear innocent, smell sweet and wet-petalled as a dreaming child under eiderdown.

So it is a surprise and a challenge to MacDougal's generosity to come up beside Drinkwater's car and Drinkwater himself, on Yale Avenue, miles from MacDougal's westend home. Drinkwater is sitting straight up in the bucket seat, hands on the wheel like a boy pretending to drive. MacDougal is startled by the mauve shadows of DW's dimpled face seized by an avid sort of smile. They say hello nice night isn't it. MacDougal, yearning to walk, feels the strangest sort of cruelty toward this Drinkwater, a trembling sadism for which he must compensate with kindness. Maybe he'd better stop and make sure the fellow is all right, looks drunk, shouldn't be driving. DW stares expectantly at MacDougal, waiting to be entertained. MacDougal becomes kinder as he is more repulsed by drunken Drinkwater. He places his hand on DW's shoulder, sends a shiver through them both. "How've you been?"

"The bloody bastards have voted for a strike. They shut me down." Drinkwater resigns himself to the soft upholstery, offers MacDougal a drink.

MacDougal's quick-sainted face, like he has seen beauty, aflame. He feels kinder toward DW, maybe he should see he gets home. Without asking, MacDougal gets into the car. The two men stare philosophically at the bare bones of Drinkwater's houses. MacDougal sees them topple and fall into dust. The sky is lit.

We are stepping
from a night
of superstition
into the full blaze
of a religion for life
and for men   instead of a religion
for death   and angels.

MacDougal sees the night's lush wing descend. He sees *the future.*

Drinkwater looks quite peaceful, nearly dignified, his eyes closed, his collar still neatly buttoned. MacDougal leaves Drinkwater in his car to sleep it off. On the long walk home, MacDougal's many voices are singing like a great choir. He won't lie down. It is a very short night. He'll write.

The Labour Church must be
the beacon
that flashes the glad message
from city to city
until the whole earth
is aflame

Turn on the Light! Turn on the Light!
Let every Worker do his Part
and the Promise of the Dawn
will Not be in Vain!

Drinkwater is damp when he wakes. It's very early, but the sky is pink and green, he observes, the colour of watermelon, Drinkwater thinks, as he removes a bug from his mouth, too early for mosquitoes. He finishes what's left in his pocket-flask. God, if it would rain right now, a cold clean rain. There's his biggest house yet, Drinkwater realizes he has driven right into what would be the front lawn. And he can't get it completed. Maybe he'll go outside for the labour. Sir Rodney has contacts in Chicago. Import enough American shit-disturbers, we could break this strike.

He backs out, drives slowly to Mary's house, up the driveway. When he gets out of his car, his trousers, his jacket, are still so immaculate, it could be nine a.m. Better to stay a little drunk today, stall the hangover. Sir Rodney is taking his coffee in the back garden, sitting at a white iron table, wearing an ascot with his smoking-jacket, and reading the Manchester Guardian. It is well known that Rodney never sleeps more than four hours a night. He greets DW without surprise, instructs the maid to provide him with coffee. "Sausages?" "Ah, no. Thank you. Not yet."

DW presents his plan to Rodney. Rodney improves on it. The plan becomes larger and more brilliant as the day's heat grows in intensity. *Bring in Americans*, yes that's good. *But bring in American foreigners*. Genius. The two men ignore the second cup, speak quietly and without unnecessary celebration of their own ingenuity. Control, it is imperative, we will not lose control.

Upstairs, a window is open. Mary is standing at the open window looking down into the garden at the sombre men. Drinkwater is the first *beau* to approach her father on an equal footing. But that's odd, he is wearing the same clothes he had on yesterday. Couldn't be. DW would never do that. He looks very well, his face is ruddy with health. Mary breathes deeply, her hands lightly stroking her satin robe, stroking her narrow thighs, her eyes on DW's mouth, his masculine chin slightly bearded, she likes his neck in its starched collar, Mary's hands stroking, caressing, wakening, *the future*. And she sees, that it is *good*.

The Canon's Diary

I spoke to Ivens today. Gave him a piece of mind my. No need for professional envy, old man like myself. Must intimidate him some. Good to be out. Different Church anyway, still yet love the of England blessed.

We met with Trades and Labour. The General Strike question must go to vote now. These are extreme measures, but I feel a strike is inevitable. Men must protest. Or is this Ivens? Full-blooded men are restless, or rather, full-bodied men are inherently restless; those were his words. Well, we have been bled.

And it is sufficient to rouse old self. Hope. I had forgotten it. In hope is the taste of happiness. They could use me and I will do as I can by them. For the new. For change. Never despair, God help me. For the new.

May 14th

WORKERS BACK STRIKERS TO LIMIT
Strike Called for 11 a.m. Thursday
KEEP IT QUIET!

Western Labour News

ELEANOR HAS DREAMED A LONG DREAM about MacDougal, dammit the man's become an obsession, I need a trip out of town, go to Uncle Rodney's cottage at Kenora, go to Chicago, go downtown today anyway, have lunch with somebody. She opens her eyes. Today is my birthday. The lonely dream recedes, echoing. She studies the mole on her right arm. She had dreamed that she'd dived into a beautiful swimming-pool, marble, empty, she'd dived gracefully into the empty pool and she swam about in air. MacDougal was there but he wasn't watching her, he was busy talking with several other men. Eleanor is grateful for the pearl grey of her négligé. The dream walks off like a dark pony. Her coffee has been placed upon her dressing-table. She watches herself drink it. Birthdays are like shells we outgrow; every year we must assess, come out naked—or wrapped in grey satin—to meet ourselves, to count the rings round our souls.

That's good. Rings round our souls. Bloody poetic. Eleanor takes her fountain pen, which is so elegant, sterling silver engraved with her initials, so exquisite in her hand, that for several minutes she sits still, sipping at her own beauty, and the lovely page, the empty haunted page. *Dear Diary*, writes Eleanor, and stops. She has been keeping a diary since her brother was killed. She hates to think that she is the only one who will ever read it, and so she imagines that it's Tony who reads her diary, lovingly, he had always been her perfect audience, laughing at her jokes before she could make them. Very nice, that trick with time, boy, she dips her pen, this is obviously a good day for writing. It must be true what they say about art and pain, whatever they say about that. Then she remembers the rest of her dream.

MacDougal had been talking to Tony beside the swimming-pool. And Eleanor had been nude, and they had watched her and their watching was touching or she was touching or wanting and wet. Then MacDougal became Tony and when Eleanor remembers this, she remembers the other thing that was unremembered for not so many years, because they weren't children when it happened and it didn't happen but close enough to make it impossible to look at Tony's eyes ever again even to say goodbye when he went to war.

Since he's been dead, Eleanor feels her height as a threat, she takes each step carefully through thin air. Where light has none of the magical qualities to hold her, walking is falling, walking is a mimicry of motion, because Eleanor knows, it is the landscape that is moving past her and she is stationary, a pantomime of a woman walking. And the windows yield to other windows, the doors to other doors, streets to streets she can't navigate, and the next moment comes out of nowhere.

> *and the Lord have removed men far away,*
> *and there be a great forsaking in the midst of the land*

And Eleanor sees the future. *And it is missing.*

May 15th

NOT EVERYTHING BEGINS IN THE MORNING. It just seems so. The Hello Girls work the night-shift too. The shift ends at seven a.m. It's been a long night and they never turn on the heat after Easter. The night-shift girls see counter clockwise—the hospitals and the taxis and the ones who don't sleep. So when the shift ends, that's the place to start, with the sun and a bit of pay.

Not pay enough. The Hello Girls have struck before. That was in '17, and the strike lasted three hours. But it got Norris' attention and he put out a lady investigator to work at some of those jobs and live on that pay and see if maybe it'd come time for minimum wage. Well that investigator started out living on ordinary wages, 5 or 6 dollars a week, and she got a room for 2 dollars a week and she budgeted her food like this:

Monday	toast	tea &	toast
	& tea	toast	& tea
Tuesday	tea &	toast	tea &
	toast	& tea	toast
Wednesday	toast	tea &	toast
	& tea	toast	& tea
Thursday	tea &	toast	tea &
	toast	& tea	toast

Friday	toast	tea &	toast
	& tea	toast	& tea
Saturday	tea &	toast	tea &
	toast	& tea	toast
Sunday	toast	tea &	toast
	& tea	toast	& tea
Monday	tea &	toast	tea &
	toast	& tea	toast

After eight days, the lady investigator fainted while she was getting on a streetcar and fractured her hip.

Put it down to the brutality of war, but something's made the Hello Girls say no. Maybe the scarcity of men makes them act more masculine. Maybe Womanhood gets stale, left too long. But it just doesn't seem fair, a woman paying her own way. Someone ought to take care of her.

Five hundred Hello Girls working the night-shift. Making connections, quieter city, hum turned down low but potent none-theless. Switchboards threaded through arteries, organized and labelled by locals, the voices entering through the headphones attached to the Hello Girls

who receive them   and give them to   you.
Wait   I'll Connect   You.

Today is the Fifteenth of May, the very centre of spring. The sun outshines the light bulbs when the girls unscrew the little electric globes that register your call. There's half a minute when their hands forget their task, rest. Then they remember. They reach into pockets and purses and drawers, 500 hiding places for 500 small pieces of cork. And they put one piece of cork in the middle of the circuitry. Then they walk outside and there isn't anybody coming in to replace them. But they've left a message: This morning, the Hello Girls are saying Goodbye.

Strike!

LOOPS OF THICK GREY WOOL, socks around his ankles, immense woollen shorts and wool vest, the hot damp stork-like figure of young Stevie, walking backwards out of MacDougal's store, pocketing his message and his tip. MacDougal watches him for several minutes, wincing as Stevie's bony knees strike the handlebars, rhythmically, carelessly. Then MacDougal pulls the shades on his shop, locks the front door behind him. He has forgotten to change his shoes, and the ones he's wearing are worn so a nail pokes into his heel. He is walking fast, the wide trousers wrapping around his ankles when he steps, quickly, past Westminster Church where several gentlemen are standing, forming a half-circle, their backs to him.

A FEW FRANK WORDS CONCERNING AGITATORS
27,000 PREPARE TO WALK OUT!

It's 10:45 a.m. Simon Shepherd, secretary-treasurer of IAM local 457, is still at work. He works carefully, always. He has pushed his grinder away from the wall; the sparks have eaten pores into the wood beams beside him. He grinds the burrs off the steel cylinder, then he hauls it across the floor on a trolley, to the welder. Back and forth between the welder, the grinder, the welder. He is very patient and his face is round, in the red heat of the shop, he has a calm face and he works carefully.

At 11:00 a.m., Shepherd removes his apron and puts on his jacket and a bowler hat. In the hatband of the bowler is a white label on which is written OBU. He tips his hat, a modest and formal salute to his employer, opens the front door of the shop, and steps outside. The street is blanched by the sun and there is a faint smell of vanilla in the air. He is followed by several other men, a gentle, almost apologetic exit.

As they walk down Notre Dame to Portage, they are joined by other men and women who walk out of shop doors and factory gates, trickling out of back alleys to join the stream, a steady increase, everyone walking quietly together, the women's skirts kicking against each other while they walk and talk quietly. Down Portage toward the corner of Main, the wide intersection crossed by telephone wires and tram-tracks. The intersection becoming an arena, filling with people now, they greet each other, embrace, shake hands, many are smiling, but they are serious, this is an occasion for warm greetings, and even laughter, but it is like other first days, when your child has arrived, or the new year, it is a day of celebration and wonder.

Not everyone has voted for this strike. And not everyone who did vote for it feels good about it. But now, it has begun, they have written it on small pieces of paper while they were working. Yes, they said, we'll all go out on May 15th. And here they are and it has begun, this strike, a life of its own.

The crowd fills the intersection and spills onto the connecting streets. MacDougal joins them down Portage a ways, arriving late and with a sore foot where his boot has cut his heel. He is limping, so when someone in the crowd calls his name and puts an arm around him to draw him in, he looks like an injured man supported by a friend.

There are rumours afloat like leaves on a river, murmuring fragments blown across these streets. *The Mayor is going to come down. See that fellow over there? he's a spy.* The woman beside MacDougal stands on her toes to see over the heads, to try to guess how many people are here, too many to count, there are thousands here this morning. It is a beautiful day. The air is full of sparrows, there is even a seagull strayed from the water, its voice like an old woman's calling her children back. It feels like summer. MacDougal squeezes the shoulder of his friend and leaves him, he moves through the crowd toward Main. There are no police here, maybe they've walked out too. People greet MacDougal, he sees them smiling, and one man with a child in his arms, the child turning to watch the limping man with the quiet face.

Now a streetcar is slowly making its way through the people. For a moment, MacDougal is walking beside it a pace. The streetcar moving so slowly, nearly stops, and the arm of the driver reaches up to the route window to place a sign there, TO BARN, and only then does he look up to see that the sign is straight, his hat falling to the cobblestones and MacDougal stooping, picking up the tweed cap, handing it up to the driver of the streetcar and the driver thinking he recognizes MacDougal, mistakes him for Ivens.

Somebody simply gets hungry and goes home for lunch. Gradually the crowd is dispersed. It's a quiet afternoon. No one gets much done today. The man with the child in his arms doesn't fix the front gate like he would if this were a Saturday, or a holiday. There is no name for a day like this. It's the first day, and nobody can say how many days there will be.

Croquet

THERE IS A PIANO. No one is playing. There is a vase of blue glass filled with Lent lilies sitting upon the black piano. A photograph of Eleanor in a plain silver frame stands beside the vase. This room has oak floors and scatter rugs. It is *avant garde*.

It opens onto limestone steps which lead to the lawn, to the riverbank. On the lawn, several young people are playing croquet. The young men wear loose white shirts tucked into blue trousers. The young ladies wear white sailor suits, seersucker. Their hair is long and bundled by red velvet ribbons.

Eleanor's shoes make a hollow metronomic sound across the wooden floor, to the stone terrace, where the resonance flattens, down the gradual stairs, to the lawn, their slight heel pressing into the grass. She puts her valise down beside the curvilinear garden, freshly spaded.

There is her father, walking toward her from the other side of the house. He is concerned. He is unable to say what he feels. He doesn't know the words. Neither does Eleanor. She has slipped out of his vocabulary. When she puts her arms around him, she is at a level with his marble-green eyes.

The handsome young people knock the bright enamel-painted balls with their mallets. They are like laughing swans. Eleanor is hot in her dark suit. Her father helps her with her bags. The driver is given directions. The apartment she has chosen has only recently been built, on Assiniboine Avenue, not far from here, across the new bridge. The driver has much to carry, and Eleanor's flat is on the third floor, from where she will have a view of the Legislative grounds.

When the driver leaves, she is sitting on the ugly ottoman in the long hallway that connects her living room and kitchen with her small bedroom. She has told the driver that she will arrange the furniture herself. She has also told him that it will be their secret. The driver has left, puzzled and too tired to care.

She has a gramophone, a new Edison which had nearly broken the back of the departed driver. She plugs it in and turns it on. Nothing. A dry click, as if the gramophone isn't real, a toy. The apartment is so quiet, she can hear someone talking on the street below. She opens the window and stands there for a long time, breathing, her breathing marking the time, numbering the voices, her father, and her brother, her relations falling from her, the voices departing from her, leaving her alone at the window looking out.

And tonight, the Citizens' Committee hasn't discovered how to give the city electrical power, and Eleanor has hauled and shoved and persuaded the furniture in her new apartment to settle into corners and be still. So she sits in the light of an oil lamp. The light is living, it sputters and smokes and it has a smell, like a candle gone out or someone who has recently left you. And it's the middle of the night in the middle of the city in the middle of May. The night palms her, she won't sleep. She listens to the light.

She has begun her reading. There are many impressive books around her big chair. She doesn't understand them. She skates over the letters, passing through quickly, lines forming and dissolving and gathering into patterns and she is losing and she is gaining, she's at the number zero, she's not at home, and it's perfect, here.

Turnip

STRIKE COMMITTEE GOVERNS CITY!
WOMEN BUY FOOD
FOR LONG SIEGE!!

But maybe the ant goes out like a wink and where's he go? My red wagon says sugersugersugersuger WANNA WANNA sugersugersugersugersuger. Am I sticky and damp, oh my but it's close. Took a bath this morning and I bathed my baby too, it'll be the last for a while we'll just have to use the sink! And the red wagon is squeaking and singing WANNA WANNA up'n'down the curbs sugersuger. One wheel jiggly making 6's on the tar and rolling over the little black ants with its hard black tires.

Turnips! They'll have to be happy with turnips tonight. And turnips tomorrow. Enough to fill a bathtub. Onions in the sink, now lemme see, if the onions're in the sink, the turnips'll be in the bath. That puts the carrots in the washbasin. No. Turnips in the bath, carrots in the bath, onions in the pickling tub. Mama had a root cellar.

Ouch that finger's blue. Tommy's a meeting poor soul. Tommy's a Committee man, my how that man talks! he can talk too! Tommy's at the meeting and baby's next door. For how long? Enough carrots to last a couple weeks. No more.

And here comes Sarah pulling her wagon too. Morning Sarah aren't we a couple of kids pulling our wagons like. Carrots! Where'd you find so many carrots? nice ones too. I got turnips. Lots of them. Come time this strike lasts dear, might come see you with some turnips that's alright. Yes Tommy's a meeting this morning too. Always a man at a meeting now.

Did you lay your sweet hands on any bread now Sarah? Oh it's fine to bake I know but flour's scarce. You find any flour dear? Not so much me neither.

Ah my, that sun's hot so soon. Stop by? Baby's gone a minute, give you a nice lemonade there's some yet. Leave your wagon here that's right, we'll sit a spell on the steps here, nice and shady too. I've a bit put away that's alright you're welcome to it. Yellow corn meal? that's nice and good for them. We can try, strain it, get rid of the crawlies and such. Tapioca flour, it is, very nice very nice for freezing I know. I recall mama using it, that's before the war.

and rolled oats and buttons of fat and spoon the molasses onto wax paper and lard and an egg and I put my wedding rings on the soap dish and I'm up to my elbows in pastry dough and sour cream with another egg and sugar and strawberries with the chicken and fat and potatoes and I can't find enough to go around and these times are thin but I know, we are doing right

Just turnip, turnip and barley and a shank of mutton for Tommy now. We'll get by and Tommy's a Committee man. There's my baby next door. You're off now, byebye, drop by you need anything, there's the baby next door, remember the turnip Sarah. There's plenty.

what we desire
for ourselves we wish for all.
To this end may we take our share
in the world's work
and the world's struggles

Church

ELEANOR WISHES MACDOUGAL would take her hand. But that would be dumb really, she looks like his big sister. And besides, her hands are bigger than his. She moves away from him so that the distance will make them more equal in size. The space quickly fills with strangers. The place is packed and more are appearing at the wide door, men in hats and loose ties. Hundreds of men, thousands.

Eleanor is happy. She doesn't belong here; she's perfectly at home, orphaned at last. Anything can happen. Now! my life is rich. No one looks at her, or if they do, something is different. She's part of something here, they expect her to take part. Damn right, she says, damn right I will.

She and MacDougal, eight feet apart, but close to the stage. The altar. This is the Labour Church, the auditorium of the Labour Temple. Someone has hauled in a small wooden pulpit. The power is off tonight. The place is still lit by low sun, and the speakers will have to shout to be heard. The faces around her, wide awake, smiling, two young men standing beside her, one with a scar across his face, laughing in such a way—with his heart.

Ivens is scheduled to speak. And some others. She has seen the names before, and maybe heard them the first time she came to one of these meetings. She doesn't know them, she loves not knowing. But Ivens: she thinks he might be mad, she's afraid of him, she doesn't care. He's standing at the pulpit. The room is suddenly quiet, a cough. Silence.

The day of miracles performed by the man of Galilee is not past. For Brotherhood is triumphant once again.

Ivens can speak like that. And he can speak about the Strike and he can even go into some detail about the Postal employees, or the returned soldiers, words that wouldn't normally be invigorating. But coming from Ivens, his enormous voice, the sense of excess, his extravagant anger, anything! the man could recite the days of the week, and get this response. Cheers and celebration. Eleanor is clapping her hands. She doesn't know how to cheer but she feels the tight moans of excitement in her throat. No one can hear, she could talk out loud and her voice would be lost in the waves of enthusiasm striking the walls of the Temple, great waves against the shore. Yes, says Eleanor into the waves. Yes.

Ivens raises his hands for silence, and indicates there is another speaker ready to take his place. He announces, *Bob Russell*, and again, the exuberant applause. And there is Russell, young, he looks almost miserable with excitement, licking his round lips, large rather protuberant eyes darting here and there, the applause still loud, Russell's large eager eyes resting on a gangly thin man with a very wide mouth. MacDougal returning Russell's intense stare. MacDougal's glance appears to have a warming effect on young Bobby Russell; he becomes more animated, his fish-like face tugged by fresh optimism into speech.

I have a Confession.

So! he speaks like a flute, a flugelhorn, has a sense of acoustics, of simplicity.

This is a Church, and so it is a place for Confessions. It is a long time since I've entered a Church. The last time I was there it was as solemn as a tomb. The shroud of mystery was over all. Everybody had

95

to accept just what the dictator in the pulpit said. But here, there seems to have been a change.

Russell allows himself to go on in this vein for only a few more minutes.

Here we discuss the issues of Life, not Death.

Then it's down to business. Russell won't be a preacher, he's a Labour leader, he's The Chief. But he's upset about the Strike Committee cards. He and Veitch had printed them up, in the middle of the night, in a rush to have them ready by the next morning so the delivery trucks could carry the bread and milk without anybody getting beat up.

PERMITTED BY
Authority of
Strike Committee

Lots of people are upset about it, and the other Strike Committee is trying to have the cards replaced.

Ivens watches for his chance, waits for a break in Russell's speech and then grabs his hand and more or less tugs him off stage. Russell has this fierce sense of self-discipline, you can see it working in him when he quits the stage and shakes hands all around. But when he sees it's MacDougal about to take his place at the pulpit, Russell just seems to forget his frustration, overcome with curiosity about the new man.

MacDougal can talk, his words are *like fire*, or is he saying *Words are fire*. Is he talking about Christianity? *The Christian doctrine of the worth of the human soul.* And he says, *There can be no doubt.* And he says, *It will be seen.* And he says, *Brotherhood is the master passion of our day.* And he says, *This is not the end but the beginning.*

And he looks into the crowd, and bends at the knee and speaks as if he is beside you in a small room, and his voice fills the big room and a great sigh runs through the audience.

The room is lit by kerosene lamps. MacDougal is searching the crowd for Eleanor, and he finally waves her onto the stage. The men lift her up. MacDougal takes her hand, finally, and draws her to the piano and he says, "Play 'Solidarity'." And Eleanor says, "I don't know it." "Then play a hymn for us." And in her terror, Eleanor begins to play "God Save the King." MacDougal lifts her arms from the keys, doing his best to absorb her embarrassment, the audience shouting No! "Play 'House by the Side'." And Eleanor isn't sure what she's playing, but everybody is singing. She plays.

Eat, sleep, play, love, laugh, and look at the sun. There are those who are anxious for the workers to do something which would provide an excuse for putting the city under martial law. Therefore, once more, do nothing. Our fight consists of no fighting.

Western Labour News

Intermission

MacDougal is walking. The city is shut down, dusty, peaceful. MacDougal is looking in wonder at his city asleep in the midday sun, thick sun-browned arm of the city, in the parks, on the riverbanks, lazing through clover, seeking, chewing, idle.

It is sufficient, to wait. Patient and satisfied, full of time, an afternoon indistinct and unnamed. The slow progression of the sun over the bridges, flat chipped shine on the two rivers. Connections made by the body asleep, the imagination a muscle, breathing and abundant.

The city sleeps By Authority of the Strike Committee. No streetcars. A single bicycle. A woman stopped in front of a market, forgetful, pushing an empty baby carriage to and fro, to. The picture show, *The Bachelor*, daylight and dust.

STEADY BOYS STEADY
KEEP QUIET
DO NOTHING

MacDougal, long legs a pendulum, hands asleep in his pockets, walks down a back lane, climbs three wooden steps and through the yellow door to the printing office, sits before his brand new Underwood, and writes his column.

The AFL, the OBU, these are more or less incidental to the great forward movement of the hour. It is ours to have motives worthy of the time in which we

"Hey Stevie! Stevie! Hey!"

Stevie. Bright eyes of a winter-bird. MacDougal and Ivens toss Stevie an envelope, and a dime.

❀ ❀ ❀

a simple sun tells a warm & yellow story in the lane where the handsome sunnybricks mumble brickdust, cobble & knuckle & yawn away because it's hot June, & the lane is long & innocent, & the footsteps & the horses & the toot toot of the new cars clamour & shine somewhere far off but in the lane, a simple summer afternoon turns its sweatered back to the radio. & snoozes.

THE MEN are excited, and many of them are anxious to "go over the top." Justice must be done, no matter how much it hurts, no matter who it hurts. The men stand solid and united for the right of workers to self-determination, to deal collectively with their employers. Let the Committee of 1000 stand in the way. The workers are as numerous as the leaves of a forest.

Anarchy

WHEN SIR RODNEY LEFT TOWN for the spring trip to Chicago, he was wearing his winter suit, not really thinking about it. So he's still wearing his winter suit when his train finally pulls into the CN station and lets him into the tranquil pool of heat downtown. He'd left Chicago earlier than expected, when he read about the trouble in the newspapers, not that the Americans were paying much attention. He'd lost his luggage in Minneapolis when the railway union workers refused to load anything heading north. So the trip up from Minnesota has been barely tolerable. It wasn't only for himself he felt concern; he was the accidental travelling companion of one elderly lady who was distraught over the loss of her trunks. She had hovered near him through the interminable trip, had recited the names of the mothers of every local boy in her congregation, lost in the mud in France. Sir Rodney had listened. He had felt the weight of his clothing, he could smell himself, a nervous odour mixed with cologne.

DEMOCRACY MUST BE VINDICATED!
Winnipeg in a State of Anarchy!

He had been in France late in '16, at the Somme. He was in London to meet with the War Office and had somehow been invited along with some other Canadian businessmen to visit the front. He'd been witness to the last Allied attack on the Somme, it happened while he was there. He watched the old woman's mouth move sideways as she spoke, her false teeth sliding, the bristly beard on her chin. Under the skin, he thought, there is flesh, it is ochre, and when it is torn violently, there are shredded curtains of blood, there is a lot of blood, even in the grisly cables of this old woman's bowels. There is much waste matter in the human body. He looked away from her, and out the grimy window to the dry hills.

The steam and urine smell of the train clings to Sir Rodney as he steps down from the train and shakes the bony fingers of the old woman. The news-stand in the station is closed. He decides to go directly to his office.

CITY FACING REVOLUTION!
Citizens' Committee Demands
Immediate Arrest of Strike Leaders!
Deport as Many as Possible!

It feels like Sunday. The streets are very quiet. He stands at the side of Main, shifts his portfolio to his left arm. It is a blessing, in a way, to have lost that luggage. *Naked came I.* He still feels the motion of the train within him as he watches some children playing on the side of the street. He feels as if there is a window between him and these events, and he watches the children play on the road without feeling much concern for their safety. They are dirty children. Sir Rodney feels vaguely that someone should care for them. But they are obviously on some kind of holiday. They are playing a game of wall-marbles between the streetcar tracks, a little army in occupied territory.

There are no taxis either. Sir Rodney begins the long trek to his office. The traffic is radically altered. *We are all one in the eyes of He who made us.* So it comes as a shock for Sir Rodney to recognize that he is in a minority here. The street is inhabited by working-people—

now that is a strange distinction, am I not *working*? In the half-hour it takes to walk from the train station to Sir Rodney's office, he encounters only one other man dressed in collar and tie like himself. Stores, cinemas, restaurants, closed. He arrives at his building. He'll call Walter from his office and tell him to come round with the car. The marble-tiled vestibule is empty and hasn't been swept out in several days. He stands in the cool shell and watches the glare in the street while he waits for the elevator. So preoccupied is he, he waits for several minutes before he hears the wind in the shaft, like a mouth over a bottle. Sir Rodney sees patches of night behind his eyes, feels the black blood pressing his skull behind his ears. He waits for the spell to pass before beginning the long ascent to the ninth floor.

WE HAVE NOT PASSED THIS WAY BEFORE
    it is the path
    of the pioneer
    that we tread today
    the new harbour of safety
    can be reached
    only by a bold
    sailing into
    the unknown
                                Ivens

Picnic

MARY AND DRINKWATER sit in the sun. They sit without anything but their own hands in their laps. They sit like that, watching the trees, the tall sky, poplars in the sun, in the squeeze of heat. They look this way and that. They squint. The light sits upon their faces, it carves the yellow-green grass upon the noonhour, the space between her fingers, the inside of her elbow, behind her knee, behind her ear, in her hair, time lingering.

They are similar in some ways, Eleanor always says, thin and perfect, no excess, except that Drinkwater's face is a bladder. They have no impatience. Now Drinkwater grazes Mary's arm while he reaches to slap a mosquito from his cheek. Mary's full white sleeve like daisies in a wind. Yet Mary sits, Drinkwater sits, blinking, perfectly shaped heads heavy between thin shoulders, Mary lifting one hand from the grass, to look at the pattern laid there. She sees the map of the lawn upon her palm, and places the hand upon the grass again. A shadow gone under the flat day. *Love is inflation, MacDougal. Never let people lie flat like that.*

Contradiction

MACDOUGAL WE MUST TALK. That's what she'll say to him. MacDougal, we've gotta talk. That doesn't sound like me. I will have to use someone else's voice, Grace's mellow, slightly aspirant voice perhaps, would Grace do? MacDougal, Grace would say, it's your turn to talk old buddy, open up. No, Grace would never do. Melissa McQueen? She'd sing whatever he said. MacDougal wouldn't talk, not to Melissa McQueen. Perhaps it is the Grace in her, perhaps it is the Melissa in her, that is keeping MacDougal from talking.

There is Grace, sitting in the pink shadow in the corner of Eleanor's living room. Grace says she envies Eleanor's apartment. She sits on the pillows, on the vaguely Egyptian rug which Eleanor bought (with her father's money) and placed there in the corner where the daylight lasts longest. Grace is leafing through Eleanor's grainy and vaporous photographs of trees and stone fences, drizzled parks, meandering rivers, solemn churches, wispy focus, formal proportions, decorous restraint. Grace has abundant brown hair, shining now in the four o'clock sun. Her lips move and her hands bracket the fibrous prints, reading the transitive photographs with a best friend's tolerance. Eleanor's poor eyesight, unsteady hand, and unfamiliarity with the developing equipment have bestowed upon her photographs an eerie beauty.

"The goddam things, they're so ladylike they make you want to throw up," says Eleanor, biting her nails.

"Your dad would love them," says Grace, and when Eleanor moans, "Elly my dear, what *would* you take pictures of? Drunks in back alleys? How about portraits? Babies Removed by Children's Aid Society. Your pictures are nice, Elly, I mean they're fine, high class. Lovely. Like you."

Eleanor swings her long foot in her chair. Grace puts the portfolio with its foliate signature on a pillow and wanders to the kitchen, saying softly, like she's speaking to herself, "You have a hard time leaving your own apartment, Elly." Eleanor hears her at the icebox, singing.

Grace is forgetful. This is one of the things Eleanor loves about her. She forgets to anticipate and expects so little, she is persistently astonished. Eleanor follows Grace into the kitchen to find her crouched at the counter eating an orange. A drop of juice on her chin, she wipes it and smiles, orange threads in her teeth. "Look at this!" says Grace. "Look at how beautiful it is!" she says, and holds the unchewed segment of orange to Eleanor. "They must have cost you a fortune!" The sticky chill of orange in Eleanor's hand. Someone at the door.

Orange in hand, Eleanor answers the door. It is MacDougal. Eleanor hasn't expected him. She invites him in, stumbling over Grace who has been staring at MacDougal as if he reminds her of someone else.

"Is this a bad time?" asks MacDougal.

"Hi," says Grace. "I'm Grace." She offers him a sticky hand. "Eleanor's best friend," she says, "except now she wishes I were dead."

Eleanor makes tea. She happens to have the crumbly rye biscuits, and a paring knife with a porcelain handle. *My miniature life, glossy and detailed. How life-like! How like the real thing!*

Eleanor is playing the phonograph; she has had it repaired. She is playing a tinny Chopin, and the garish notes scrape against the quick sharp flagrant light.

"You must be exhausted," Grace says to MacDougal.

"Why is that? Oh. Yes, it's busy. There are many people involved of course. Takes some of the pressure off." He helps himself to cheese. "This is awfully good. Feels like the strike never happened. Up here." Eleanor listens for reproach in his voice. But his voice is neutral.

"So how are you making out on your own?" he asks Eleanor.

"Oh fine. At least I think it's ok. I should find work."

MacDougal looks at her, an indeterminate glance. "Why would you do that?"

Eleanor's kettle shrieks above Chopin. She bangs her head against the sloped ceiling. She is always banging her head up here, unaccustomed to low ceilings. When she returns with the tea, Grace and MacDougal are laughing over some story it appears Grace has told. MacDougal rarely laughs like that. Eleanor wonders why Grace is exempt from MacDougal's impatience. But no, MacDougal is never actually impatient.

Eleanor is wishing MacDougal would go. And come back. She would love to be missing MacDougal. Go Home, MacDougal. Come Back. She listens attentively, not hearing a word. MacDougal is listening to Grace. And the air, slow. MacDougal, studying the brown, the egg-shell, careless Grace lying on the pillows and MacDougal looking into her, his compassion covering her, becoming her.

The Canon's Diary

18th May   and hot to spark a fire

What joy to be alive, to see a world born new from the old corpse of our shameful past!
From nightshades, from my dreams and memories may the Good Lord deliver my soul.

I wake and I feel and I know this feeble shell, my shattered old man's body shall live! Quickened at this hour of liberty!

The streets are full of men. I do enjoy a parade.
Seize the seize the day, boys! We shall be one sentence me To Life!

It kindles my heart. And to recall, how we were lost in the fear and the mud and so many young boys killed, so much blood. Bobby Ferrill's leg. No one, not even my own flesh, looks the same, ever again. When it is dead. When it is a part.

Let me die in peace, knowing no more self murder. We shall be one with what we lost to fight. We shall see a better world. It is coming. I have faith.

Beauty.

My old soul is full of praise tonight. It will be difficult to sleep. She would sit up with me, on nights such as this. She was a great companion. What a mind the woman had, though she thought with her heart.

Revolution

"I'VE ALWAYS ADMIRED YOUR HANDS," says Eleanor, lifting one to her cheek, a hand white as soap, long-fingered, polished nails boat-shaped and ivory. Cool against Eleanor's long face, MacDougal's hand, she tests it, rests her head against it, the hand doesn't resist, she returns it to him. They are sitting on the divan with the Jacobean table unfolded and covered with a tablecloth, with Eleanor's white china. She has cooked dinner, a Bourguignonne, the first time she has ever done this, with quite a lot of good red wine in it, and quite a lot of good red wine in Eleanor too. Has MacDougal had anything to drink? Is he bored? Should I talk to him?

The silence is the most potent silence Eleanor has ever lived in. She endures it like a kiss. She is at that stage of intoxication where what used to be clumsy becomes artless and candid. She will tell this MacDougal something, she will make him listen. What will he want to hear? She asks him questions about himself, but the liquor has made it difficult to listen. She wants to talk, to make the final statement, utterly perceptive, practically clairvoyant.

She thinks she hears a trace of the Clydeside, the thick burr in MacDougal's rrr's. But he says so little she can't be sure. She wonders how she might make him say something with lots of rrr's in it, Royalty, or rapture. He asks for a cup of coffee. How foolish, of course, wait a minute. She is happy, she smiles in the kitchen. Surely MacDougal is happy too. But maybe he would like to talk about the books she has been reading. She has a thousand questions to ask him, but she can't remember them right now and that's too bad, the ideas slipping away from her, and it had been exciting, reading the past couple of days, like hearing the ocean for the first time, just beyond.

She walks through the shadow of the unlit hallway, to the living room, to MacDougal who has picked up one of the heavy books beside Eleanor's chair, he's thumbing through, thanks her for the coffee, takes it black. She expects him to ask her about it or tell her something about the book, she is sure he has read it, it's his field, isn't it? But he doesn't ask and he doesn't say, he puts the book away and walks to the window, which is open to the night, and Eleanor thinks she might grow wings she's so astonished to see MacDougal put one step upon the windowsill and climb out, disappearing into the dark.

There's a low yellow moon near the bridge. MacDougal's shape against the amber sky. He is crouched on the roof which is flat enough and big enough for two. He doesn't help her clamber out which is fine, it's much easier out here in the ambivalent comfort of MacDougal's silence. The trains are running tonight.

Recumbent. A Word

And tomorrow, she will stand in the middle of every room, astonished, deliquescent. She can't concentrate.

                    She knows
                 what his hands
           feel like
    (soft)
              she is so in love
                 with him
                    she can't read
                       she doesn't know
                    what happens
                 to her
              with him.

can i?

CAN SHE? Can Eleanor take MacDougal's clear-polished and slender hand? Draw him down the long empty hall (past the photograph of her brother) towards the yellow light of her boudoir? Her sulking-place. (She has placed a map of the World above her bed; no Renoir for Eleanor.) Will she speak to him as they walk, Indian file, trailing each other like circus elephants? Will she say the most accommodating things: a butter-yellow earthenware jug beside her blue bed, the tusk-white cross-stitch. A pleated marriage of form and content, fold of a wimple, fret of a lute.

Can she undress him? Will he undress himself? Can she look into his eyes as she unlaces and unbuttons and slips her dress from her shoulders? Ah! Will she see him? The consonantal chesthair, the oily smooth tissue. Will she be seen? Is it enough? To say, her breasts, they are, they are, her breasts, they are soft, and beautiful. Can she touch him? Can her fingers follow the unfolding? Would she run her long middle finger from his forehead, into the cavetto of his throat (he is silent), would she obey the symmetry of corpus callosum between the two hemispheres, harmony, unison, plumule? A feather boa is an original sin. Can she? Corpus delicti. Our joyful delay. Nolens volens. Wilfully.

OLD ART, SO BOWLEGGED he only wears out one side of his boots. He's got a house outside town on Number 6. And a barn, and 20 good horses. People come out from the city to ride at Art's place. Because it's not too far from town. In fact, Art can see the big city buildings any day of the week. And at night the clouds turn pink with the lights. But tonight, it's like his house has been moved far away from anywhere because even though the stock did settle and his grown son went home, and the sun did set and the long sky slept in a bed of crocus, and Art set himself on the big gate and he looked across his yard and the road and the thistles, even when the nightdark lay in the bush, the lights of the city don't come up. It's the first time since the city got electric lights, Art hasn't looked out and seen the city warm as hearthstone. Never been so many stars in a night.

The labour men have the upper hand, and so far as they can, are showing Bolshevik methods. Mounted Police have come to the city, several thousand men are drilling and in readiness for any riots.
From the diary of the Rev. Dr. John Maclean

Citizens

THERE IS NO DOUBT ABOUT IT, Drinkwater has great organizational skills. How he contrived to have these people together on short notice in this place, well, it's anyone's guess. The food's good here too, they serve a great brunch. DW did the right thing when he ordered ahead of time; who could argue with Eggs Benedict and these butter rolls?

He should work for somebody's election campaign. That will likely happen, next election. Some candidate will snaffle him and bango! he's got a second career as party boodler. His brain must work like a social directory. Because he really knows the right people, he's got the touch.

Just look at this crowd. Winnipeg's finest. And they brought their wives. People with a conscience, people who care about this city. And they're not here to blow their own horns, they're not here just to be seen. In fact, most of these gentlemen have agreed to come to this meeting on the condition that their names not appear in the Press. They don't like publicity. They want peace, and prosperity. Their only desire is for a quiet family life, and fairly liquid assets.

There's Mr. W.R. N— , he's with the Wholesale Grocers Association now, formerly with the Retail Merchants, a brilliant man, and very generous; he has just slipped Drinkwater a promissory note for $5,000. And over there, behind the column, hard to see him, but that's Dr. F.G. S— , representing the Medical Society, $2,000. At the table beside him, accompanied by his lovely wife and junior partners, Sir J.A. O— , K.C., senior partner with L— , F— , A— , and A— , $3,000. And Mr. T.O. B— , the Real Estate Exchange, $1,500. And Mr. W.A. M— and Mr. B.I. F— , the Builders' Exchange, $4,000. And Drs. B.M. W— and A.W. W— , the Dental Society, $1,200. There's more. It's very moving, this show of support, a great day for democracy.

But it's not just the money. These gentlemen are here to give their time, too. General Ketchen strides to the centre of the dining room, nodding and saluting, waiting for everyone to notice him. Then he lets the room fall into a respectful silence before his broad leather-boot voice says, "Loyal-minded citizens! we are in need of your support. . . . " The upshot of which is, the General requests these athletic gentlemen, golfers and tennis players one and all, to join the militia, "to uphold constitutional authority," which is to say, Don't panic but if the Reds won't listen to reason, get your gun.

It isn't all so glamorous. The Committee of 1000 has taken responsibility for providing some of those essential services of which we are deprived by this invidious Strike. Even before the breakfast dishes have been properly cleared, Drinkwater leaves Mary and a hot cup of coffee. And he doesn't appear to be the least bit self-conscious when he shakes General Ketchen's hand and surprises Dr. R— by taking his coffee spoon and tinkling it gently against his water goblet, the sound we usually associate with wedding guests' desire to see the groom kiss the bride. But it works: people stop mid-sentence, and they're quick to realize that it's time to get down to business.

DW and Sir Rodney have it all worked out in advance. They've segregated those public services paralyzed by the strike. Following the advice of General Ketchen, they've made a list of sub-committees to look after different services. And some duties aren't much fun, but that doesn't stop the Citizens from offering to do their share. It will all be run out of the Board of Trade Building. DW and Sir Rodney and some other key players will run the headquarters there, organizing the various teams. It's humbling, to see these professional men take on the menial tasks. Mr. A—   , LLB will take charge of the milk depots, and his son Gerald will be running the bread deliveries. From the Builders' Exchange there are a good number of engineers to run the waterworks. And the fire brigade. And the street cleaning. And the garbage collection.

And a small, elect, able-bodied core of young men, returned from service, who have taken the table under the great window through which the early light tumbles with such optimism, who have eaten such an amount it has tickled the dedicated hotel staff to see their appetites, who are still in uniform, young officers now at university, a thick-trimmed red moustache, a clean-shaven face, a round one, a thin one, solemn they are, and proud, and somewhat remote, they sit together, smoking, eating their enormous meal. They are here to see that Justice is served. They are present because they are the sons of the Citizens, the city's future. They offer nothing less than Themselves. They will personally patrol the better neighbourhoods, to protect the daughters and wives and mothers from thugs and aliens and revolutionaries. Through the uncreated night, the keen rugged eyes of the restless young soldiers, watching, walking the silk-lined streets.

CHOOSE BETWEEN THE SOLDIERS
WHO ARE PROTECTING YOU
AND THE ALIENS WHO ARE THREATENING
The Winnipeg Citizen

But Mary, who has spilled a little red currant jelly on her white kid purse, is suffering from her all-too-familiar nervous disorder. Only this time it's worse. She and Eleanor are sitting like perfect strangers at the table by the doors, with Sir Rodney and Eleanor's father. The cigar smoke is making Mary sick. The stewed eggs sit like blood-shot eyes on her plate; she moves it away—*when* will those frowzy waitresses remove this debris? She sits with her back to DW, and though her father is facing her, he looks right through her, thoroughly engaged by the excitement in the room. Even Eleanor. Look at her, twisted in her chair, unblinking—why, she's not even here! Mary studies the fragile skin around Eleanor's nose. She isn't thinking anything, Mary decides, or if she is thinking something, it's irrelevant.

And Mary feels the tension in her wrists, her hands are cold and they ache. She notices that the cuticles around her fingers are dry, and when she tries to push them back the small motor action fills her body with irritation so that she moans without meaning to. It awakens Eleanor, who blinks and looks at Mary's left ear. Eleanor turns in her chair, grinding her knees against the tabletop as she tries to arrange her impossible self in the frail chair. There is a new quality in Eleanor's movements, a slack sort of indifference; she slouches, her shoulders are round. Mary could put her aching hand on Eleanor's shoulder-blade, the bony plate sticking out of Eleanor's strange flimsy dress (a glittery lamé, better suited for evening), she could lift the blade from the back, peel it off like a piece of chicken or a fin. Eleanor puts her elbows on the table, exaggerating the dorsal fins on her back, she crouches over the remains on her plate, licks a long finger and presses it against the crumb-littered tablecloth, sticking the finger into her mouth. And as she chews the white breadcrumbs, she becomes aware of Mary's attention, looks up sharply at her cousin, the two women staring at each other, smile, on the off-chance the other might smile back.

117

We are under the sway of Bolshevism in the city. Everything is quiet, but there are some ugly rumours floating around, and the Home Defence Guards are all ready for action at a given signal.
From the diary of the Rev. Dr. John Maclean

Toy

IT IS THE WAY THE LITTLE WHEELS go around that fascinates Eleanor. The miniature connecting rods and driving wheels, steampipes and chimney, and a chip of crystal for the headlamp. It fits in her hand and the thin driving wheels roll across her palm, like tiny claws. She caresses it as she might a living thing. It's made of tin, malleable, very shiny. When she holds it against the last bubble of sunlight, she can see right through the windows in the cab. She tries to show it to MacDougal, but she can't hold her arms straight because of the jostling of the carriage over the mud road. He doesn't notice when she slips the little train into his pocket.

They have half-circled town, skirting the mute city, MacDougal watching always on his right. They move from the west to the north, MacDougal watching the city to his right, Eleanor admiring the sunset. And when the radiant sky has fallen, laid down pigeon-greys, they take the road to the east and now the light is behind them.

MacDougal says he has to work tonight. The three big newspapers shut down today; the stereotypers have joined the strike. Now there's only the Labour News. Eleanor knows MacDougal goes to the Labour News offices because she saw him go there once; she was meeting her father at the bank to sign some papers, something to do with her brother's death, and she had seen him cross Main in front of their car. He had waved to them, his scarecrow figure flinging an arm, and Eleanor's father had said, "It's my guess the angelic fool is on his way to the Temple to sing his praises to the Reformation." Or the Revolution. Something like that.

She doesn't like to be out at night anymore. They are heading home. They are between two dark places; the black cushion of farmland is behind them now. They know they've reached the city limits when the horses stumble a little, their shoes on the cobbles, kettledrum. Sporadic lights here and there in the buildings and houses, people staying indoors, or walking in groups, someone holding a lantern. From a dark house, yellow light coming from deep within—the kitchen perhaps—from this hollow dark house runs a small child, spooked apparently and chasing a parent out to the street, calling, "Wait! Wait!" and the high-pitched voice rising over the subdued streetnoises, striking the buildings, echoes waitwaitwait.

"I'd like to see this editorial room, if you don't mind. That is, I could get my own way home from there, somehow," says Eleanor, and she thinks, it's like jumping into dark water. Maybe MacDougal had already chosen to take her there; smooth as a song, the man is, but sometimes I think he must be autistic. "Hello?" she says as MacDougal is climbing down, absently taking her arm to steer her toward the back door. "You know MacDougal, I sometimes think you must have been locked up in a cupboard when you were a kid. There's something strange about you." "In a cupboard?" says MacDougal. "Fred! You're working late."

Fred Dixon, Eleanor remembers him. He is the most comfortable man she has ever met. When she was introduced to him at the last meeting, she'd instinctively leaned against him as he spoke to her. And she was being cautious. What she'd yearned to do was put her head against his chest, maybe fold herself there, weep and tell him why. Very carefully now, she offers to shake his hand.

Dixon says he's glad to see MacDougal, and they sit down on the desks nearby. Dixon has read MacDougal's column and he's excited about it. The room has a bare wood floor and has been painted a tired yellow. It's new, the building is new, the dust is new. Eleanor has the feeling she's chewing dust, it's in her eyes, the evening is choked with it, dust in the mechanisms of a clock. She is unsettled, would like to take notes, something to do with her hands. She is aching. And time sitting on her like ruffled feathers.

MacDougal and Dixon are talking about the police, who appear to be in a fix, caught between their own Commission and the Citizens' Committee. Dixon says the police have been given some kind of pledge of loyalty they have to sign—they have to make some kind of vow. Dixon says it's not really the Police Commission but the Citizens' Committee who need it. Eleanor is sitting in one of the swivel chairs, and she's swivelling and scribbling on a notepad, listening in a fragmentary way to the men talk. She has recently discovered (and maybe this discovery has given her freedom) that she can indeed listen in a fragmentary way, skipping like a thin stone in and out of these conversations, alternating her listening with a conversation that she has begun with herself. In this way, Eleanor has discovered, she can listen and place the fragments that she takes from the men according to her own translation. And another thing: it doesn't matter anymore that her patterns of translation differ from MacDougal's or her father's. The men speak their public language, and it is a marvel, their absolute sentences, and Eleanor, living under and between, always outside, has a place she can furnish according to her own design. She has decided this is good.

And now the Citizens' Committee needs to know the police love them. They want the poor solid cops to promise complete and utter fidelity. Or they'll all be fired. Dixon is saying the Citizens actually *want* to fire all the cops because that way, they can bring in *Special* cops, ones they can be sure will be sympathetic to constituted authority.

They've left the door open. They all hear the step and turn to see a thin boy's face appear in the skittery lamplight. His face is mostly ears and forehead, lit like a little moon, and his smile cannot be innocent, but it is faraway, inspired by something other than these dusty events. MacDougal rushes to greet him, puts his hands on the boy's narrow shoulders, bends to eye-level, says, "Stevie's here!" Turns toward Eleanor and Dixon, pushing Stevie before him into the office, "Here's Stevie!" and he is convinced this fact will give the rest of the world immense pleasure. Dixon is amused, shakes the boy's hand. MacDougal has the papers ready, bundles them into Stevie's arms and when he reaches into his pocket to pay him, he finds the little train. Eleanor starts to explain, takes it from MacDougal and gives it to Stevie who accepts it with the same limitless, wondering pleasure with which he has received all the bounty of this funny strike.

Stevie on the Bridge

ON THE MARYLAND. River blue. Brown looking right down at it, but the wind chopped up into little waves. Crowds of passerbys passing and me and ma talking and I give her a hand with the parcels she's got too much. Green everything. Heads on bicycles bobbing up and down. Ma says it's a peach of a day and I say it's a circus like. Or flags and kites, balloons, red round faces. All, allalong the river and over the bridge.

And I say Look! Look ma! and she looks and me nearly running into the back of her dress both her and me stopped like this and she's grabbing my neck pulling my head into her stomach like I'm just a baby and I jerk free. Gulls garbage eater birds screelingscree can hardly hear some old rich guy hitting his cane on the driver's window, What's all the ruckus? English fart. When ma yanks me off the road only trying to get an eyeful sos I get up on that ledge thing there and ma holds my legs.

And geez. Hear it in my heart first. Bababoombabaoomba and the chocchocchocchoc marching. They're marching grand and their arms swing alltogether. Holy holy mother of ma starts to say think she'll choke off my windpipe lemmego ma I say.

But how they walk their boots and hats tip in their eyes looking not to me or not anybody. Straight. They shine straight. And fast their hands swing kinda fast fisted white. Ma and me saw them today and now I never can get asleep.

B & E

SIR RODNEY'S IN HIS WORKSHOP, a well-lit little room in the cellar, wonderfully cool tonight. Mary loves the smell of the basement, moist, doughy. This smell is defeated, however, by the visceral stink of her father's workshop. He's in there now, likes to work late these days. He hasn't been sleeping well in the heat.

"Daddy how can you work with that stuff when you've got the door closed?" Mary's reprimand, and her excuse for barging in on him. She kisses his ear and fondles her favourite soldiers—her father's miniature reproduction of the Battle of Waterloo. Mary loves these best, the red uniforms, the little horses; her favourite is a beautifully reproduced Napoleonic soldier half mangled beneath a handsome white horse ridden by a Prussian in blue.

"Why do you insist on that tedious bunch of modern stuff? Those grey uniforms, they're so depressing."

Rodney's latest series is his most difficult. The moulds aren't available and he has been forced to produce his own. It will be years before anyone reproduces the Great War on a large scale. So, with a diligence that has indeed made him sombre of mood, recalcitrant, even irritable with his Mary, Sir Rodney has worked many nights till the birds sing, at a miniature reproduction of Vimy Ridge. Mary gazes at it mournfully. All that *grey*. It's *disgusting*.

"Daddy," she says, putting upon his name, in her lightsome way, the hint of a British accent. "I'm going out to walk Muffie. You don't mind do you?"

Sir Rodney's forehead is slippery, glows in the light. Doesn't look at her. Nods. Mary's relieved that he doesn't realize she's going out so late, again, tonight.

There's another thunderstorm. It's still very hot outside, the leaves are bouncing and clapping with rain. The sky looks like it has been shelled. The ground shivers and the street is shocked blue. Mary ties Muffie to a tree a few houses away, and gives him the entire back rib from the roast. Muffie is happy.

Mary calculates, every second resident of Kingsway is at a summer home, Winnipeg Beach, Minaki, or Kenora. Their houses are absolutely deserted; they've even taken their servants with them. It's a good way to keep their household help quarantined from that Bolsheviki flu. Only the really stuffy loyalists have remained. Bully bully.

She knows exactly which house she'll hit tonight. The Squib-Avonhersts' on Harvard, a great big square thing, a house beyond reproach and totally unremarkable, just square and classy, like a top hat. And it's completely dark. Perfect. Mary walks around to the back, relishing the privacy. The moment is so right. She remembers the back yard from when she played there as a little girl, exasperated by the prickly afternoon sun, waiting for her mother to have tea with the ladies. Poking around back then, she had discovered the little screen door that led from the summer kitchen to the stables. It had been open then, but of course, the house was full of people that day. But maybe, tonight, she'll have some luck.

She tucks some lily of the valley into the buttonhole on her wrap. Here's the screen door, dark brown bubbly paint, it's unlocked, and—so is the inner door. Mary is in the summer kitchen, standing on the cool quarry tile, sniffing the oatmeal air, lightning splashed across the pine furniture. She is humming the Hebrew Benediction; it reminds her of a christening, all lacy and crisp. Humming cheerfully, Mary walks away from the servants' quarters through the padded pantry door, into the dining room, which is so dark she can barely bump her way out of it. Cursing the Squib-Avonhersts for their Victorian tastes, and very nearly upsetting the salt cellar, Mary trips into the vestibule and finds her way at last to the front parlour. She stands quietly humming. In the blue flare of sheet lightning, she examines the fine handiwork of the bronze hinges on the enormous French doors. These people really have the most unctuous taste. Oriental pots everywhere, and art nouveau till you choke. And they still use those awful crystal lamps. Re-volting. And oh lordy look now, they have the old family Bible on the organ. It's so Dutch.

Mary sits in one of the smoking-chairs under the front window, light shattered by the stained glass in the transom, relaxing, sits with her legs straight out and her arms fallen either side. Her hand wanders blindly to a wicker basket beside the chair, seeks the spaces in the weave, her little fingers poking into the basket. Suddenly, Mary jumps out of her chair, tips over the chess table, and returns to discover the grotesque hairy thing in the basket. "That's sick!" In the basket is the little terrier, once beloved by the lady of the house, and stuffed now, kept in the parlour, on its haunches, begging.

Mary is so indignant, she feels justified in lighting the coal-oil lamp at the foot of the bannister, quite a pretty thing actually, glass blown into a rose-shape. By its bony light she sees her way into the sunroom, Mrs Squib-Avonherst's domain, delicate cane furniture, more Japanese prints, the glassy room sweet with the exhalations of Mrs Squib-Avonherst's orchids. Mary sits in the spoon-backed chair, arranges her skirt around her, and leans over the porcelain jardiniere that contains the pouting lady's slippers. Breathing in so fully, Mary must open her mouth, she takes the bloom between her teeth, bites tenderly and pulls away, chewing thoughtfully.

WHO WILL GET THESE JOBS?
ALIEN ENEMIES OR
WAR VETERANS?
The Strike Committee's Answer:
Starve the Babies
So Aliens Can Get Their Jobs
Winnipeg Tribune

The Special

ELEANOR DOESN'T TURN ON THE LIGHTS. The power has been on in the city for some time, but she sits in the space cleared of dark by candles. This has affected her habits, of course. She can't do much by candlelight, so she's likely to sit aslant in her chair, her head tilting to one side, resting her head in her hand, listening.

She speaks in paragraphs, long and short ones, alternating eddies of the fictions she's rewriting. The diary has become an embarrassment to her, though she keeps it on the kitchen table and she writes brief cryptic nuggets, a couple of lines to mark the place where her private monologue surfaces, the too-graceful markings of an adaptable creature in her new environment. Sometimes she speaks aloud between the silent paragraphs, she says, "I'm sorry." Or she says, "I love you." When the rhythmic exchange blossoms into one of these verbal captions, she walks about the apartment, down the long hall, into her bedroom, looks out the window, takes a brief tour of the kitchen and back to her chair. But she stops, now, before the photograph that Father took of her brother. It is dramatic, half-lit, the collar is a crescent under his jaw, and she looks at him and she tells him, "You're dead."

The summer sky is purple. The apartment is still hot, but there is a wind so she takes a cup of tea out to the roof. Dark city, the lighting plants providing only partial power. Footsteps below. She breathes and blows on her tea. No, there are two sets of footsteps and one is running. Not toward but away from something, fast. She can see him running now, that squared off fast run, chest squared and hands fisted. Chasing him, the other man runs on his toes, not so fast, confident. From behind the hedge across the street appears a third man, and he heads off the runner. Now there are two men against one. They take him into the park that runs along the river. Eleanor can't see them for a minute and she considers going down to look and she thinks in her next life she will be a large man. Then they reappear, walking, their hands on his elbows. They keep him between them. Eleanor has never seen a beating like this, not even in the movies. She hates all three of them, especially the victim, his flesh splitting, his voice, the fact that he doesn't say anything, but the sounds he makes shouldn't be uttered. He is the only thing between herself and the men who are beating him, and he is failing, and she is failing him. They let him go, he drops and rolls into himself like a caterpillar. They separate, one of them walking quickly toward Eleanor's apartment, wiping his hands.

He has put his hands in his pockets, and comfortable this way, he looks up. Eleanor has moved to the unsafe edge of the roof, toes in her shoes clutching the tiles. Crouched, she sees him through her knees, and he looks up as if she has called him. It is a perfect greeting. It seems to Eleanor that he must know her very well. Then he walks on, out of sight under the eaves.

Her tea is cold and tastes like a penny. She goes inside. Still hot in here. She takes a soda from the icebox and turns on the electric light. It's not good light, she hasn't yet acquired good lamps; these ones are overhead with opaque glass shades. Very thorough lights. From her chair, she has a view of the living room and the front doorway. The back doorway is in the kitchen and has a double bolt; she rarely uses it except to hide the garbage no one will pick up, and she puts the dead plants there. She must go downstairs and find the man who has been beaten. She is afraid of him more than she is afraid of anyone.

She has left the front door open because of the heat. The telephones still aren't working, not at night, no one will volunteer for the night-shift. How long has she been sitting here? She has to go downstairs and cross the empty street to the park to find the man who has been beaten. Her fear becomes a very big and empty room. She is looking out the window, searching for the figure on the grass. She'll go down now.

She is turning to run downstairs when she sees the strange man with his hands in his pockets, standing in her doorway, watching her. She has had many dreams of this, the ones where she can't find her voice. And it is a lucky thing she is mute, because it gives him a chance to walk into the apartment, and take off his hat, holding it in an obsequious way before him, a posture that has always confused Eleanor, the hired-man pose. She is standing in her apartment *receiving* him, not a threat or an enemy, and not exactly a friend, but an *employee*.

She is not very good with names. All of Drinkwater's associates look alike to her, well-made. They are named Robert, Charles, or George, and they are all eminently harmless. They go to university and then they graduate and they work quite a few hours a week and they keep in shape, swimming and playing a bit of rugby. They have no argument with the world.

This young man is so familiar, it is like looking in a mirror. He has an original face, an extreme version of "classic" good looks: the upper lip is thicker than the bottom one, heart-shaped, hair cut very close to his head, big shoulders. They are difficult to see, but he is wearing rimless spectacles. He must have removed them before the beating. She looks for cuts or bruises, sees his knuckles are bleeding. He is different, after all, from Drinkwater's fluent poker players. She asks him to sit down.

"I'm sorry. I've forgotten your name," she tells him. She is restless, hasn't decided yet what to do, she must go down to the park.

"Wes. Wesley Salton. We met at your father's house last Christmas."

"I remember. You're a friend of Drinkwater's? You were in the service. I remember. And going back to finish university."

"Still am. Do you mind? Do you have a drink about the place? I'm feeling a bit off."

She does. Presents it to him in a Waterford glass, Port, too much like blood. She has some too, it doesn't go down very well. "We should, or I should, go and help him."

"No, don't. Someone will show up and take him out of there. He wasn't alone."

"Who is he?"

Wesley, absentminded, licks the blood off his knuckles. "Five of us, we're working shifts, since the strike. Six bucks a day. And one of our guys is a real hothead. I mean, I didn't know we were going to get Loyalists on our patrols."

"Is that who you beat up?" she asks, peering through the window. She can't see a thing.

Wesley is alarmed that she could get it so wrong. "No! Why would we do that? I mean, we're on the same team."

"Sorry."

He is patient with her. "No, you see, the man we—beat up, like you say, he was writing stuff all over the fences, your neighbourhood, near your dad's place."

"You fought with him for writing?"

"No. With paint, red paint. And on one place, over near McQueen's, they'd written all down the side of his stable."

"There were a lot of them?" Eleanor wants to know. *In our neighbourhood.*

"But when we get there, we see maybe 15 guys, strikers, and they start chucking rocks at us, bottles, rocks."

"Six bucks a day. You're working for the Citizens' Committee."

"Not exactly. We work for the Police Commission. I don't know if I'm going back, after this."

"You're a law student. I remember, you were a friend of my brother's."

"61st, three years." Wesley Salton says this mechanically. He says it often these days, when people want to know what it was like *over there*—not much to tell them in so many words. He's more interested in his local brawl. "I didn't sign up with the Specials so I could get involved with this sort of thing. I mean I just think somebody's got to look out."

Then Wes says, "We hurt him rather badly I expect." And Eleanor is suddenly so relaxed it's like the first wave of sleep coming over her. Wesley speaking this way, the civilized phrase, "rather badly." Yes, and we feel terrible about it and it's going to be all right. She says, "You must have been very close to my brother, after three years."

"Yeah. I'm sorry. A stupid accident."

Wesley expects her to agree so he doesn't look at her for confirmation, doesn't see her standing precariously. "An accident."

Wes sees her and he says, "It was one of ours. Exploded prematurely. Faulty shell."

"Oh."

"Thought you knew."

"No."

"Well." Wesley looks miserably around her apartment. "I guess it isn't my night."

So. He was killed by accident. One of our own shells. It must have gone off pretty close to him.

Wesley has this tragic air about him. Eleanor sees that he is about to leave. He's standing, mournful, at the door. It must be very nice, to walk about on a cushion of tragedy. It's very attractive, too, he must get on well with the girls. She locks the door after him, no more Specials tonight.

And it seems, as she creams the salt from her face, splashing the water in the chipped sink, these collisions are written in red paint on the stable door, bright paint on fire against the night. She takes care to wash her face, and she sprays perfume on her wrists so that she can hold them to herself and fall asleep in fragrance. Tomorrow she will go out and see these things for herself. She will take care of herself, she's going to sleep, and eat breakfast, and go out. There is a black background and we are moving against it, setting fire against the night.

Did your Washerwoman Show Up on Washday? Hasn't the Strike brought Home to you the fact of how Dependable a Time Saver Electric Washer would be in your Home? Think! Your washerwoman is asking 40 cents an hour and you can't be sure she's coming. And the Time Saver Electric Washer is Always at your Command, costs 2 cents an hour to operate, and will last a Lifetime.

Winnipeg Tribune

Cabbage

THE HEAT JUST WON'T STOP. The garbage collectors are out on strike and the Mayor has told them in no uncertain terms "they have created a condition that is not at all nice." It's not so bad in River Heights, of course, but downtown! Whew! Mary gags, gets dry heaves, driving in her open car, dodging great heaps of stinking garbage. She's not much of a driver, the car lurches and stalls right beside the very worst maggoty pile and young Mary is burping and clammy when she finally gets that car going and out of there. She decides to take a breather and drives directly to the City Hospital to visit her friend Lauren, who is a nurse of all things, though she doesn't even have to be. She rids herself of her car and walks carefully across the lawn. No flowers have been put in, and the place looks dreary and awful.

Fat robins jerk across the empty garden. Mary wonders how they can move like that, so quickly, like little machines. This thought makes her feel more queasy, fat machine-birds seeking worms. She'll ask Lauren to give her something, some soda water to settle her stomach. Then she sees a ladder against the grey brick and a young man in shirt sleeves who has just removed the storm window. He descends with the heavy wooden frame just as Mary passes and he says, "Would you take this from me? Thanks Miss."

Mary thinks, *doesn't he realize I'm not well?* And she stands still, staring at this very rude man. He says, "It's not dirty, I promise you, just cleaned it." He's smiling and Mary understands, there really is no malice. Gamely, she puts her handbag on the grass and lifts her arms to receive the storm window. She holds the bottom half while the man climbs down and then takes it from her. "Thank you kindly," he says. "You're a sport." He is the very best looking man Mary has ever seen. Is he Italian? He has that fine-boned masculinity that Mary thinks might be Mediterranean. A foreigner! He gives Mary a brief intense look and returns to his work. Tipsy, she almost forgets her purse, returns for it and then says, reckless, "But you're on strike." The young man turns, surprised, "You're right!" and shifts the ladder to the next window. Mary runs to the hospital and stays with her friend Lauren until she's sure the young man has really gone.

So it's late afternoon before she actually begins her odious errand. The sun is still hot. Her little respite at the hospital hasn't fully restored Mary's well-being; the antiseptic odours have made her feel so ill that she knows she would go home if she weren't afraid to do so, empty-handed. And just as she was sipping her soda water and telling Lauren (who was distracted, indifferent during Mary's recitation), just as she was telling Lauren how difficult this strike has been for her, the orderlies came along with their big trays of food—Mary was astonished, do people really eat *dinner* at 4:30? And such food! She lifted the cover on one of 50 trays stacked outside the ward: stewed everything, and canned peaches, a glass half-filled with milk, the sides of the glass coated with cream. Hands trembling, Mary returned the cover, sipped her soda and studied a basket filled with soiled sheets. Time to go.

The sun is so bright, so hot. She grinds into first gear, and her car wanders down Bannatyne, she's always had a good sense of direction anyway, thank God for that, turns at Sherbrook, due north. She's never been to Mrs Sokolov's house, but her father drove that lady home once when she'd come down ill during a work day, gave her the rest of the day off too. Mary remembers it, Mrs Sokolov fainting in the kitchen while she was heating Mary's soup and her father had whispered to Walter that Mrs Sokolov was probably pregnant, again, and Mary had shared her father's disapproval because after all, how could these people afford so many children? Mary is pushing backwards into the leather seat, trying to relieve some of the restriction around her stomach. She remembers Mrs Sokolov's rudeness, her resistance to Sir Rodney's solicitations; Mrs Sokolov had raised herself from the kitchen floor, biting her lip, tears behind her glasses. Nausea can make the most ordinary memory seem unbearable.

She finds Mrs Sokolov's house. It's tiny, quite charming, the little front yard given over to what promises to be a vegetable garden. Quaint. Mary carefully closes the front gate behind her. She feels much better, everything so clean and *nice*. She is knocking at the rather badly chipped front door, the house isn't nearly so well kept as it looked from the road, and disappointed, Mary smells something awful emanating from Mrs Sokolov's kitchen. *Cabbage.* Mary loathes cabbage, such a smell! Mary must return home, she is so sick, now with this chipped white paint and the *cabbage*, she pushes open Mrs Sokolov's front door. Inside, darkness, shapes moving, a woman wipes her hands on an apron, comes to greet Mary, enters the sunlight. It's Mrs Sokolov's oldest daughter, Mary met her when she came to help with the cleaning last spring. "Come to get your maid?" she asks Mary, quite gentle, this woman.

Mary says, "I came to see you. I'm sorry I've forgotten your name." And Mrs Sokolov's daughter declines to name herself, says instead, "Your father's packing plant shut down."

Mary is startled. "I've forgotten your name." Mrs Sokolov's daughter declines again to give it, but waves to Mary to follow her into the little house. But the place is full of people! So quiet! "I'm sorry," says Mary. "I didn't mean to interrupt."

These are young women, Mary's age, slouching on the couch, feet up, fanning damp buttery throats, cotton skirts hoisted, but still booted and laced. They are stopping here perhaps for a meeting.

Mary nearly panics when she sees there are so many. She had thought she'd appeal to Mrs Sokolov's daughter, what is her name?, appeal to her as a daughter, please, let's mend the fabric of society, come back to work, we'll pay you fairly. Mary had imagined this meeting, she, wearing something simple and white, raising her hand in a pledge, come back to work, we need you.

It's not going to work out like that at all. Here are these women, they sit up sharply when Mary arrives, smooth their skirts, some of them stand, formal and awkward. What language do they speak? Some of the women laugh, Mary sees their faces, broad features, so different from the narrow noses, little button noses of her old friends, their teeth are bad, they smile to each other, glance at Mary.

Mary speaks loudly, in consideration of their foreign tongue. "Would you like work?" she asks, framing the words, slow, bold. Mrs Sokolov's daughter—her name! her name is Lydia!—Lydia is walking out to the kitchen, but she stops dead when she hears this. Turns to Mary, *such a look on her face*. Mary focusses on her desperately, "Lydia, we can give you work!" And Lydia, graceful as a pendulum, swings back through the room, takes Mary to the door and deposits her outside. Mary is standing on the porch alone, and within, the house seems so private. She feels the mysterious presence of Lydia and her companions sitting silently in the house.

"Well," whispers Mary, stepping carefully down the untrustworthy stairs. We all have our sororities. God! That smell! When I get home, I'm going to drink Pinkham's in the bath. And eat chocolate. Then I'm going to wear something nice. And go out tonight. Yes. She will go out tonight.

Home

It is late afternoon before the meeting breaks. MacDougal offers the Canon a ride to his home. The Canon doesn't comment on MacDougal's mode of transport, but gratefully he takes his place beside the younger man, and he observes, the new hotel has changed management, then he settles to the squeal of iron on wood and the oily breath of leather and the slow progress of the horses who are wheezy and he and MacDougal comment on the health of their lungs, a bit of wind, call the vet, maybe.

The Canon asks MacDougal if he has been well. MacDougal has. Very. Ah! it is refreshing to hear. And you are still in your apartment, it is above your bookstore? Yes. Comfortable? Quite. And MacDougal, feeling rather careless, tells him, "I don't require much in that way. I have been alone for perhaps too long. Set in my ways. Old dog new tricks isn't it?"

"You have been recently acquainted with a very good friend of mine. I do hope I'm not stepping beyond my bounds, my son. But you see, Eleanor is a favourite of mine."

"Yes. She is a fine woman. Yes. I've been in her company. That is, we have become acquainted."

"She is going to be a woman of complexity. If she can keep up her strength. Women with her rather peculiar ambitions sometimes break down. It is just too much for their constitution."

"She will have the support of her family, will she not?"

"Yes. Of course." The Canon saying this as if he is out of breath, suddenly fatigued. He watches the familiar houses with affection, it seems, or his eyes water from looking too long. He resumes. "She has taken a residence of her own, I am told. You see I am in contact with her father. He is concerned, of course. Astute. And not without sympathy for our cause, mind you. But he worries over Eleanor's enthusiasms. Many young people of intellect have taken risks with our ideas. She will need a guide, you see."

MacDougal smiles briefly. It must be the strike. He had forgotten this old style of ministry. He welcomes the Canon's intrusion; he warms himself in nostalgia while they ride. The Canon is humming loudly. And he had forgotten how it is to be with an old man. Full of song and echo, and in their strange ways, permissive.

"That is the way for some women," MacDougal says. "Looking for herself in a marriage, I imagine. I don't think I've got the strength to remake her. I feel that she is waiting for me to invent her anew."

His carriage, the motor-cars passing quickly, the breeze in the trees, the Canon's pebbled voice, "She is a determined and independent lady, mind you."

And MacDougal, speaking to the paths through the leaves, "I think a woman like that will always be homesick."

Rue

WHEN ELEANOR WAKES, her room is ash-blue. And the taste of dried grass in her mouth, and the wind blowing through her hollow bones, it blows night dust and last night's words through her frame. Long, in the bruised dawn she lies.

MacDougal has left. She can feel his hands on her, he had dipped his fingers into her and she feels them there. She wonders if he had liked the feel of her, like apricots, like dried fruit. And then.

And then he left while she was sleeping. He has left her with her own scent on her hands, sweet mulch smell, and when she closes her eyes, sun under hollyhocks and his warm hands on her belly cool as earth in the shade.

And finally she must rise and bathe and begin again. Today is Wednesday. And what does it matter that she has a bath? And when she goes for a walk, she will say hello to strangers. Hello, they will say, Good day. Because in this world we are safe, we hold each other gracefully and we dance, one-two-three one-two-three, knowing the steps of the one-two-three, carefully our arms holding one another, apart.

On an empty stomach, she walks part way to MacDougal's bookstore. She will walk a while, and then she will walk back without stopping there, stopping short of a reunion with MacDougal, whom she supposes she should call her lover, now that he has touched her and she has touched him this way. And before she is aware of it she is singing

> *of mercy and judgment unto thee O Lord will I sing*
> *I will behave myself wisely in a perfect way*
> *O when will thou come unto me?*

But she does walk to his bookstore,

> *I will walk within my house*
> *with a perfect heart*

and halfway up the stairs and stands still as a hummingbird without saying a word. There is a picture in the stairwell between MacDougal's suite and his bookstore. It is poorly done, a primitive sort of thing, lathered in oil-paint. There is a ship in a storm and aboard the ship, red-robed priests, Catholic types, Cardinals, Bishops, that kind of thing. In a panic, they appeal to the purple heavens for salvation. Drowning in the cobalt meringue, black-haired men and women, hands clutch helplessly, the smooth brown surface of the hull. It's obvious, the priests have a rosier future.

She is studying this picture and fighting a wave of vertigo, when the door opens above her and MacDougal is standing at the top of the stairs. He is neatly dressed, collar and tie. She can smell his familiar soap smell.

"My lord, you gave me a start!" he says, and comes down to meet her.

A fathomless space opens between them. He stands beside her on the stairs.

"Awful thing," he says, "I've had it since I was a boy. It used to give me my most memorable nightmares."

Eleanor would like to scrape a wave off the painting with her fingernail. Her mouth is full of saliva. MacDougal places a warm, fraternal kiss on her forehead. He holds her elbow to steer her downstairs. Eleanor's short laugh like a crow crying elsewhere.

"You're looking trim."

"You're looking trim too."

MacDougal seeing Eleanor with eyes that haven't memorized a shape; Eleanor feeling herself growing larger and her vast body glass-blown and protuberant. Eleanor seeking an avenue in the maze, she would conform to MacDougal's vision, if only he will stay. Still. Long supple arms tucked to her body, Eleanor raising her hands to his face to supplicate his kiss. *He is so generous.* His eyelids shut by themselves. Kiss like a sudden light. He is tired, she guesses, I know what that is like, when company stays too long.

Boulevards

The delphinium have grown too long. Their irregular blue spikes are staked. And yet, they topple and break.

She stops at the small store on the corner and buys some chocolate and when the sweet flat brown fills her mouth she nearly drowns in the memory. She seeks out the stray strands of MacDougal with that terrible obsession over past moments, he said, he said, I said, then he said, and how he looked and he loved me then I'm sure, reliving, relighting the errant sun.

The Right to Remain Silent

But when I see those uniforms, I really want to scream. There's something about a man in a uniform, makes me mad enough to hurt somebody. But we really gave it to those bastards. Yes, we did.

CLOUDS TODAY. AND STICKY. It won't rain. The rain won't come till this strike's over for good. There's rain in the air too, but it won't come down, just stick there smacking and sucking the glue out of you.

Nobody says anything, they just stand there by the side of the road, waiting. Nobody's dressed up like they would to meet for cards and a soda summer nights when the kids are down at last. Not today. They're really quiet. Essie makes a joke of course but there's a feeling generally it's not a good time to joke. Some are here because the husbands are home from work, and some are here because the husbands don't *have* any work, but some are here because there are no husbands, just work, and the boss says he'll pay them a family wage but there isn't any family just them and the kids, and the kids are skinny and everybody's always tired. One of the ideas is they stick together because they're all alike, the women, but what happens is, they're together because of their differences. It makes them quiet.

Then they hear the trucks coming. How those women know there'll be trucks coming down this afternoon, nobody can say. But

141

they're better organized than the press knows. And they've got guts. And they've got the mad anger, they do. That's not just the property of the men.

Two delivery trucks for the big store downtown. Helen's been stopping the female clerks at the door early mornings this past week, and she's had good success, she says, lots of the retail girls joining the strike. But that big store just brings in scabs from Toronto, and pays them better than their honest employees. It's made the women mad.

Kind of hot flat sunlight pressing them down to Arlington Street, the garbage still lying there stinking and the sides of the road all filled up with gum wrappers and the kids' loot. The grass lying dead as old hair, boulevards going bald in the heat, and the place not cleaned up after the winter and after the war. You look down on the brown grass and there are 50 shoes, scuffed and flat-soled, pigeon-toed and otherwise, all of them eager to kick somebody's ass. And here come the trucks around from Portage Avenue. The drivers must see the ladies by the roadside, but everybody's so still and whispery, maybe they think they're going to get a sandwich or something, a mug of beer for their efforts on the part of the 1000. Then the ladies move themselves across the road. And the drivers in the two trucks just slow down, and the guy in the first truck's still hoping to nestle through like a man at a dance, maybe flirt with the housewives through his truck window, give the ladies something to think about in bed. So he just rolls his window down with this smirk on his face and shifts his cigarette with his tongue to the side of his mouth so he can talk, squinting in the smoke, big faced beefy jaw, neck like a ham, must weigh 220 pounds anyway. So is *he* surprised, when Tressa just stretches one hand up to the cab and sticks her fingers in his mouth and yanks the lips on the face to one side. He's so shook he steps on the gas pedal which of course makes it the worse for him because Tressa has about four fingers with those long painted nails of hers stuck in the side of his mouth so he's kind of helping her then to pull his own face apart. And the truck behind can't see what's up, though they must be getting a fairly good idea they're in for some kind of fracas now. The second driver gets out of his vehicle and that's when somebody throws a rock and his windshield shatters the way it should, the other guy in the second truck, he's going to stay in there, gets down on the floor of the cab, but he puts one hand on the horn and starts blowing, no idea who he thinks is going to help a man out in those circumstances. But the fellow who got out of the truck probably fares the worst. Irene has a piece of steel pipe from somewhere, she swings it like a baseball bat across his face, twice like that till he goes down and then they kick him and it's either perfectly quiet only with the sound of the women kicking him or that sound is the heartbeat gets them worked into coordinated harmony, like they know when it starts and when it reaches its middle and when to gentle down, go back home everyone and see what happens next. They don't slow down till the two trucks are wrecked and all the store merchandise is ripped out of the back and spread all over the dead grass. Then Anna jumps inside, all that glass and that, she doesn't give a damn by now, she gets the rig going and several of them jump aboard and away they go out of town with it, going for a joy-ride, arms about each other, but no one looks happy, they have peculiar faces, between a yell and a cry. They let the drivers go though, somehow they get away before they're killed.

And later, a detective is sent out to discover just who was responsible for wrecking the rigs, but he doesn't get anywhere.

"I wouldn't advise any man to go out there," he says when he gets back to central station. "His life is in danger if these women find out he's been working during the strike," he says. "They don't respect police officers either. They do anything they damn well please."

Pale Wandering Baby's Breath

MACDOUGAL IS RESTLESS, he can't work, he can't write. He has begun a letter to a Brother, but the words have wandered off and begun their own litany elsewhere, blown like the topsoil from the fields of his imaginings. He has begun one book and another, but surely there are more important books to read, and all the books he hasn't read are calling, calling, Read me, they say, Read me too.

The wind blows, the air is full of elm seeds like snow, the children in the street lift brown bare arms in the scarlet heat, It's snowing! It's snowing, they cry.

Across the thirsty river, Walter wonders if he should bother to plant the vegetable seeds or set the wilted seedlings in the garden. It's so dry the garden is brick-checkered. Walter's trowel spoons up old soil clumsy as clay, a cupful of clay to a cupful of spindly oldskin roots, smell of mud. Hollyhock, sweet william. And all the seeds and all the seedlings whimpering from the paper bags, Plant me, they say, Plant me now!

And down the street Eleanor remembers last night's meeting, under the stars, the rhythms of revival, *MacDougal*, she says, *MacDougal*.

The Lake

MARY ALWAYS SLEEPS IN THE VERANDAH in the hot weather, never before
so early as this. Such a steamy spring, ripe as summer. Mary is happy
to sleep in the verandah, on the hammock suspended from wrought
iron, on an apple-green mattress, under a yellow throw, propped by
six embroidered pillows, the cottage reclaimed from mice, bats, and
squirrels. Walter's been quietly at war, barricading, trapping rodents,
to fortify Mary's rustic domain.

She usually wakes at dawn in the summer, lies in her satin nest
to watch the sun petal through the earnest spruce trees, sunshimmer,
coffee-coloured shadow, and beyond, the big glance of sun on early
lake, still, always perfectly still in this hour. And then she curls her
hands under her chin, curls her back upon another sleep, dreams of
fish like stars under water.

Daddy isn't here this weekend. And another blessing,
Drinkwater's coming tonight on the train. This is good. What's also
good: he leaves again tomorrow morning. She'll put him in the main
cabin, not the bunkhouse this weekend. They'll stay up late, she'll
dabble in petit point, he'll stare into a book, then she'll beat him at
cribbage. Walter can cook them something too rich to eat and late,
after hours, they'll go into the big kitchen to cook some eggs. Good.
Mary's good with eggs.

Mary rises at ten. Stupid woodpecker. Can Walter shoot the bird? Where is the man anyway? She wraps herself in her mother's peignoir, combs her hair with her fingertips, takes a croissant from the breadbox and leaves by the kitchen door, tiptoes because the stone path is still cool, into Walter's little cabin on the other side of the point. She digs in his kit bag till she finds his Red Cross socks, the brown ones, her favourites. She hates to wear shoes at the lake, and it's really too damp to go around bare just yet. Walter has an icebox in his cabin, lucky thing; well supplied too, beer, back bacon, a round of Stilton, and a pomegranate. Mary takes the pomegranate.

The morning sun is on the rocky point. She drifts through budded birch, her peignoir is scallop-pink, she plucks a seed from the pomegranate, sucks the syrupy flesh. She arranges herself on the warm rocks, the lichen crumbly silver. Leans on one elbow, hurts, god this rock I need a blanket. What to do? A white-throated sparrow sings the first seven notes of the *Fifth Symphony*. The drinking sound of water against the rocks beneath the dock. The dock might be more comfortable, damnation, I'm not going to get all nervous today am I? Mary takes the arm of a little pine and follows the narrow shore to the dock. The boat! She'll sit in the boat, on the fat damp cushions in the warming sun and eat her breakfast and listen to the sparrow and the loon.

The boat is 24 feet long, mostly bow, and it's narrow, nine feet in the beam. A needlenose. Nice. This boat is the *Elizabeth*, named after Mary's mother. The *Lady Elizabeth*. It's a Minett, and the only one at Kenora. Daddy had it built for him specially four years ago. Mary drops Walter's socks on the dock and leaps gracefully to the needlenose, youch the wood's hot. Her toes trace the shiny brass screws, she climbs over the windshield, swoops onto the leather seats, hot, Walter must've removed the tarpaulin hours ago. Settles into the long couch in the stern and nips on the seeds from her pomegranate. She is murmuring, her pretty voice gentle, clear, she murmurs, *This is a Minett. It's 24 feet long and I like it best when it's tied up. It's made of hand-selected African mahogany, hand-rubbed with ten coats of varnish and a blend of stains. It has a Chrysler engine and it goes 12 knots, but only Walter and Daddy care about that. It has triple chrome-plated brass fittings and fawn-coloured leather. And one day, it will be mine.*

The Canon's Diary

June the first

That such feelings may exist between us is a mystery. Perhaps I recall myself in him. I was as gangly as he, though we are wiry in our own way. My health was good, as a boy, whereas Steven looks pale. I imagine there isn't enough at home. I've met his mother. Anna is her name. She is a good woman, hard-working and even-tempered. But it's hard to provide for four. There is never enough to go around.

He is an odd boy. A real boy.

I have well rested. I feel his youth this morning. I hope I am making myself useful around here. I do what I can and I would like to be of service. But up he'd look straight to my bleary old and we'd smile. Such a smile in a sparrow, a youth.

No matter how great the provocation, do not quarrel. Do not say an angry word. Walk away from the fellow who tries to draw you. Take everything to the Central Strike Committee. If you are hungry go to them. We will share our last crust together. If one starves we will all starve. We will fight on, and on, and on. We will never surrender.

Ivens. *Western Labour News*

Millennium

Hot words? *Poppies on the fields at Flanders!*
War makes sweet mulch for words incendiary and prophetic.
Let there be an end to endings! Our joy shall be in beginnings! And hereafter sentences, they shall be anterior appositive. And forever shall reign the supreme and elliptical logic of paradox, that the brother of low degree may rejoice, exalted.
Good wives! Seduce thy men by virtue of your virtuous ought. We will be encyclopedic in our love of otherness. Noun phrases shall be our making, nouns fraternal, and even unto the prostitute and the drunkard and the thief. Love shall be our noun and our verb and loving our gerunds, so by naming them we exalt the All, in lengthy sentences of doubtful grammaticality.

and in our words, red
as the poppies and blue
as the dead
shall we invent relief
for the destitute
the neglected and delinquent children
relief for the sick
for the inebriate
the aged, the crippled, the feeble-minded
the widow, her children, the children, relief
for the children

Marx

. . . making it possible for me to do one thing today and another tomorrow, to hunt in the morning, fish in the afternoon, breed cattle in the evening, criticize after dinner, just as I like, without ever becoming a hunter, a fisherman, a herdsman, or a critic.

THE BELL WAS ABOVE THE DOOR when MacDougal bought the shop. It used to *tinkle* when anyone came in, a lacy noise, frail and merry. MacDougal tied pinecones to the bell, and now he doesn't hear Eleanor when she enters. His back is to the door.

She ducks when she enters the shop, something to do with the light. She is suddenly in a hurry. She's got on a pair of shoes she bought in England just after the armistice. They've got rubber soles and thick flat heels and they're quiet on the wood floor of MacDougal's bookstore. And a new plaid skirt, with lots of give around the knees so she has been able to walk here from her father's house, at a dog's pace, taking big steps and walking on the dry boulevards where her shoes made no sound. Her right foot toes in, she discovers, when she walks, makes her feel innocent. Wonders why she hasn't noticed this before.

MacDougal turns around. Must've heard her coming. He offers her a chair. She sits on the edge of his desk. Bad move. She sits.

"Such a beautiful day," she says. "What are you doing?"

MacDougal motions to his desk. "Much the same. The New Order." He pushes his chair back. "I think I've finally got hold of it though. It's nearly too quick for me."

"Who is it for? I mean, when it's done."

MacDougal leans back and rubs his chest. Eleanor loves the way men do that, grabbing their chests and stretching their arms, so at home. He smiles by way of an apology; Eleanor wonders if she'd asked for one.

"Us. That is, all of us. If I can reach them."

Eleanor likes this idea too. Reaching. She reaches for a book beside MacDougal's handwriting. "It is inspiring," she says, hands holding her book. "Not just you. I mean it's all so inspiring. If there could be. If there could. But I don't see it, MacDougal. My father . . . dammit, I say that every time. Every time I go to say something, I sound like the goddam Lord's Prayer."

MacDougal stands up, shaking off Eleanor's joke, but smiling, and his smile, a chastisement. "I like him, your father. There were a lot of men like him back east. Frontier sophisticates, exiled aristocrats. They spin a good yarn and call it Empire. That's all right, of course. It has brought us this far." He stops, reined in.

"Yes I know," she says, "but I don't quite see it. You're right, naturally, I mean of course. But I just don't see how. Well some things can change without our hardly noticing. Poverty, for instance. Oh. I guess not. Dammit." Bites her nails.

Eleanor Capitulates

She tells him she's been home, that is, her father's home, and she's found the old neighbourhood fixed up like a garrison. Her dad isn't so foolish but he says many of his neighbours are sleeping with guns under their pillows. She tells him these domestic miracles in a high-pitched tone of wonder. She has never been good at knowing what people want. The story of her old home under siege, she would like this story to be *received* by MacDougal.

He looks very tired, splotchy. He shrugs and rubs his eyes and then, taking turns, he tells Eleanor a little story of his own.

MacDougal Finally Tells Her Something

I have a friend. She is a nurse. She has been seeing the strikers' families for free.

One day, my friend was very busy because there'd been an outbreak of chickenpox amongst the children in one particular section of town. She went from house to house and everywhere she found the families living in "utmost poverty." That's a nice expression, don't you think so? "Utmost."

On this day, which was last Monday, the children hadn't anything to eat. Their father worked for one of the iron companies and he has been off since the beginning of May, but they were very poor long before that. In fact, he'd emigrated from Ireland when he was a little boy, and his mother had died on the way over. There is a pattern developing in this story, but I'm sure it's not lost on you, you have become so well read.

Anyway, on this Monday last, my friend the nurse entered a home on a street you've never seen and she found the family very hungry. They hadn't eaten since the day before. With the children being ill in the night, their mother hadn't slept, and hunger and fatigue made her seem confused and listless. She was sitting on the bed beside the stove and her children (there were eight children) with her, they were very quiet.

You know what chickenpox looks like? It is a democratic disease, perhaps you have suffered from it yourself—yes I see one small scar on your temple, somehow it contributes to your beauty, being one flaw to remind me of your perfection. That's Browning, isn't it? Anyway, these children were very sick and their sores were infected because they were so unclean.

So my friend began to wash the children and to apply an ointment which she had brought. She intended to get them to the food kitchen somehow, after cleaning them as best she could. She wasn't surprised that their mother didn't respond to her and she was really too busy to notice much until she had finished with all but the smallest child who was sleeping in its mother's arms. She spoke to the mother who seemed to be comatose. But it was only when my friend tried to remove the child that she realized that they were both dead.

"Well. That is a sad story, MacDougal."

"Yes. I'm sorry."

"No, you don't need to apologize." As there is nothing much to add, Eleanor stands to go. She doesn't know what to do for the mother or the child. She knows many women of her own class who attend to *the poor*, hauling boxes of food and used clothing to the north end of town, returning south long before dark. *Let me in,*
there are places in your
heart where I could live

MacDougal is silent, *obstinate son of a bitch*. It isn't like I'm always after sentiment and luxury, I'm not Mary, for christsake. Look at me. I'm trying to leave myself behind.

"Well, I'll be going then."

And MacDougal asking her, "Would you be free, would you want to help out at the kitchen? They need people to work."

"Yes! Are you kidding? What kitchen?"

"At the Oxford. The Oxford Hotel."

"Well sure. When?"

MacDougal writes down a name, hands it to her. "It's run by the Women's League. Get in touch with Helen."

"Yeah, I can do that." And she leaves, tipsy; this must be *enthusiasm*. Call Helen? Sure. I can do that.

154

The Free Press has installed a wireless on the roof of its building so now we are all right, and the strike is practically broken, as the working folk have no money, and they are sick of the strike.
From the diary of the Rev. Dr. John Maclean

A Young Man with a Future

SOUND TRAVELS WELL OVER WATER, Mary knows, sound travels well. Over the dark lake, the men's voices, amplified, clear and low, their resonance and authority clearly evident to Mary, who sits in the dark dangling her feet into the black water. She splashes her toes in the inkwell, drawing jewels in the night. Only the caress of light wind, the chipped paint on the south side of the boathouse rough as a cat's tongue, the taste of pine in her throat, and the voices of the men who have cut the engine and drift, now, just off the point. She sees a match flare and a white shirt cuff, cupping a pipe.

They don't know she is here. But then, it wouldn't matter if they *did* know. She will sleep upstairs in the boathouse tonight and when the moon rises, it will shine through the screens and there will be fingerprints all over the room.

She likes that man Alby or whatever. Our M.P. The one with the pipe. He has a leathery, pipe-smoke smell and he never gets excited like poor Drinkwater. She is comforted by Alby's—or whatever—his voice, she listens, leaning against the slow words. His long, balanced, confidential sentences, the gentle persuasion, implacable as limestone, the broad granular tones. And he is humorous; hear the brief melody of the men laughing quietly at one of Alby's mild witticisms. With a bit of luck and a lot of hard work, DW might turn out like that one day. I should tell Drinkwater to take up a pipe.

Mary is sleepy. She won't wait to say goodnight to anyone. She won't even go upstairs to wash. She slips out of her dress and slides down the ladder to the nape of her neck and she treads water a moment, her legs scissor slow her arms pushing against the abrupt cold lake. Then her feet on the turtle-slick steps and up to the dock where she stands dripping, and it's amusing, to be invisible. To not say goodbye, but to retire like a closed moth on the lip of night. She will climb the steps to the bedroom above the boathouse and listen to Alby the M.P. teach Drinkwater rhetoric, and she won't worry about anything, she will sleep in the timbre of Alby's graceful sentences, she will leave the evening ajar.

Alby's elbow cracks when he bends his arm to light his pipe. It is the same sound the boat makes, the varnished creaking of the wooden seats of the new Peterborough. Sir Rodney and Alby in leather boots, which drum heavily on the trellis, and Drinkwater wearing light Italian shoes, cork soles, good for boating.

"We'll keep the ones who appear to be suitable for the work of course." Alby's voice has a strange effect upon Drinkwater; it resonates in his inner ear, it echoes in his own diaphragm. When Alby speaks, those who listen to him respond with lowered voices, to match the broad masculine tones.

"We'll supply at least another hundred volunteers by tomorrow morning, am I right Drinkwater?" asks Alby.

"We'll have 150 men there for the morning shift. Sir."

The Peterborough lists to starboard when Alby moves over to one of the cushioned seats and makes himself comfortable.

"How do we get them into the post offices?" Sir Rodney wants to know. He has seen how difficult it is to keep control of these situations, when even the most careful planning gives way to the arbitrary events of a moment.

"They'll arrive early, by about an hour. They'll already be at work when the picketers get there."

"Then we drop it on them." Drinkwater relishes the summary; it's like a successful end run.

Alby approves. It is encouraging to meet a young man who is perceptive, and discreet. "That's right. They have a choice. They can return to work and forget this union business. Or they can forgo their jobs."

"Well, it has been a very difficult decision, but I think we're moving in the right direction with this," says Sir Rodney. "It has the added advantage, if one considers this from a compassionate position, of providing the employees with a noble option, that they might honourably disengage themselves from the criminal, that is, these radicals—who I might add strike me as being somewhat sainted." The men laugh together, gently. "In fact I'm quite serious," Sir Rodney continues. "They have a way of living above life as it is ordinarily lived. I could almost say I envy them." And again, the affectionate approval from his listeners.

The slow current has drifted the wood boat to the south of the boathouse—Mary can't hear them any longer, she has fallen asleep. Lulled by the nightbreeze and the sounds of their own agreement, the men don't realize that they've floated against shore till the hull scrapes a little against the rocks. Drinkwater chuckles and casually he takes an oar to push them off. Alby sits up and he ties his bootlace, speaking into the fine ribs of the boat, and he says, "It will save the government and the public a good deal of money."

DW respectfully asks him how this might come about.

"Well they lose their pensions," explains Alby. "It's a fair omen, I think, to start fresh."

WE WENT BACK TO THE BOARDING-HOUSE after that, and he left me there
so he could go out again, I don't know where he went. I wanted
him to hold me and it's always like that, wanting him just when
he's walking out. I lay down to sleep. God that place stinks. Papa
must have found some money because he was sleeping loud. A
whole family in there, partly mine. Smell's so bad we keep the door
open onto the hall, and the light on out there keeps me awake,
shining in my eyes, shining in my dreams, and the dog piss and the
cat piss and the old magazines and one sock rolled off a baby's foot.
I lie on my belly with my chin on the pillow. All stopped by wanting
him inside.

I think I might as well get up out of bed and see what the night's
doing. And there was Joey my little one sneaking home up the fire
escape. Joey my favourite. He's only 12 years old. I'm harpy with him
tonight. I've got this heart like a badger, seeing my little Joseph with
blood on his face, muddy and mean, turns into a song to sing me
awake. Well away goes Joey (after telling me to go to hell). I'm in
nothing but my slip and the iron stairway cold these nights thank
god. I can see the city streets almost pretty, trees look new, full of
leaves. And I put my own hand on my own breast and it doesn't feel
so old.

Some nights nearly meet your singing. But then I see them walking, him with his arm under her holding her steady since she'd been drinking I know. She fits him good. She's younger and nicelooking from the side. She doesn't have any kids yet. On the grass she goes on her knees in front of him and puts her arms around his legs. He's standing there swaying soft and his hands on her hair forgiving her.

He turns up at home a few times after that. One time I throw a breadknife at him but it falls flat on the wall. I never could throw worth a goddam. But one time he comes home I cry for him. I miss him and I haven't been touched till my skin's like invisible and my stomach and my heart going to fall out of me. Because he's so different now he's with her. I wonder why I love him better when he's stranger. But that's not why I'll get him back if I have to kill her. If I had a thousand wishes it'd only be I wouldn't need him back for nothing but love. I know I can't hold him. But I can't feed these kids on no pay. I need a man's earnings. I'm getting old and there's nothing else to do.

Liberty

INSIDE, IT IS VERY COOL. White, the blue water, the lights at the bottom of the pool. It is early morning and there are not yet many children. Three young boys, obviously brothers, play in the pool. It appears their greatest pleasure is in entering the water. They crawl up the side of the tank, chasing one another, and slip back, splashing and laughing hard enough to drown. MacDougal is watching them, his eyes follow feet upon slippery tile, he watches the faces of the three boys.

Eleanor puts her hand on his arm in an attitude of urgency. She speaks closely into his ear, to make herself heard above the noisy children. They are standing, Eleanor leaning toward MacDougal as if she would pour her words into him. And MacDougal's brown eyes following the children in the water, taking in her words, uneasily.

Eleanor reaches the end of her supplication, and repeats it, almost to the word. MacDougal's eyes flit for a second from the children to her face, back to the swimming boys. Eleanor's hand, moving from his arm to his shoulder, speaking closely into MacDougal's ear. As she speaks, she studies the soft waves of his hair, her eyes trace the curls on his head, curl upon curl.

At last, it is the mannerism, the voluptuousness of Eleanor's repetition that wakes MacDougal. He shakes her hand from his shoulder and steps over the film of water toward the boys, his impassive face broken by joy. The brothers know him and clamber out of the pool to tell on each other, they shove and tease and MacDougal's face is wet with the water, his face is a moon reflecting the lights from under the water.

And only later, when she is alone once again, in the privacy of her apartment, as she folds herself into her reading-chair, does it occur to Eleanor that she might have helped MacDougal with the boys at the Mission pool. She might have taken a white towel from the shelf and thrown it over the head of the littlest brother, scrubbed him and sent him off with the others to climb outside to dry in the sun. She might have joined MacDougal in his care of the children. She can't remember what the boys looked like. She remembers the cool white chamber, and the way their voices had sprayed. Incommensurable. In a mist.

Parade

MARY WASHES HER FACE in the porcelain sink, runs the water hard and long, knowing her father can hear it from his pillow where he is reading in the next room. She brushes her teeth with baking soda, the clean sting on her tongue. She pulls her blue silk bathrobe over her blue chiffon dress, carefully tucks in the collar so nothing is showing, puts her nose to the closed door of her father's bedroom and says, "G'night Father." Sir Rodney says, "God bless."

For three hours, Mary sits in her armchair by the window, soothed, drowsy. Then she tucks her shoes into her pockets, rumples her bed, knows the stairs creak worse beside the bannister, carefully misses the last step, steals through the pantry and down the back stairs. The night is lilac.

Drinkwater's car is idling on Yale. Mary hides her bathrobe behind the caragana, runs barefoot down the driveway, and there is Drinkwater sitting in his roadster smoking a cigar, his short brown hair rumpled and boyish. Mary runs toward Drinkwater's car, hating Drinkwater for looking rumpled and boyish tonight. She fumbles with the stupid door and has such a lump in her throat, she can't say a word when Drinkwater flicks his cigar and turns to her. He looks about 12. "I fell asleep for a while," he says, "thought I was going to miss it." He smells of sleep. Mary, falling into the seat beside him, can barely endure the regret, it makes her dizzy. Drinkwater has discovered a perfumed scarf in the pocket of the side-curtain. "For your hair," he says, "my mother's." Mary wraps the scarf around her head, leaning against Drinkwater's shoulder, delivers her revulsion to the breeze. Too late, too late, better to love young Drinkwater now. They drive through the dark streets, Mary watching the canopy of elms over the road, the green moonlight, a solitary man walking his dog. They drive west to the outskirts, to the Tuxedo Military Hospital, restless hotel for 225 vets. There are more cars, maybe 25 or 30 shining motor-cars, waxy and gorgeous in the June night. They make a huge racket. All of these cars are empty and for some reason, all of them are running. Drinkwater leaves his car running and Mary in it. He enters the yellow glare of the hospital. The galaxy of motor-cars rumbles and stinks. Mary is nauseated by the time the men begin to straggle back. Drinkwater is among the last, and with him, two young men in uniform. Very gallant, they hand crutches to Mary and wriggle into the rumble seat. The two soldiers are probably younger than Drinkwater. He introduces them: Jimmy Dunn is the one with his left leg blown off just below the knee; Bill-Somebody seems in one piece, and Mary can't tell what's wrong with him.

"Good," says Jimmy Dunn, sitting directly behind Mary. "We're getting an early start. Makes me think of home. We get up early you know."

"Funny," says Bill, trying to read the faint lines of Jimmy's face, "I still like a parade. I do. I wonder why." Bill combs his thick moustache and Mary can see his hand, no more than a claw, the skin like roasted poultry. He begins to sing, a voice narrow as a water snake, gliding through the artillery-noise of the elegant motor-cars moving down Academy Road.

> Johnny, get your gun,
>> Get your gun . . .
> Take it on the run,
>> On the run

163

Mary has been taught to drop everything, listen ardently when someone is performing; that's how it has been when her father has invited a little orchestra and that rooster of a soprano what's her name to one of their dinner parties. But she has never heard anyone sing like this before. Bill is a tenor, and when he sings this sweet melody he stretches his long neck, his lips caress each syllable, his eyes run with tears, his thin face is wet with them

we'll be O-ver, we're coming O-ver,
make your mother proud of you,

pack your kit,
show your grit

Early dawn makes the buildings blue. Drinkwater pulls into the big lot behind the Hudson's Bay. Jimmy Dunn leans his big knees into Mary's seat and he says anxiously, "Thought we were going to Victoria Park."

Drinkwater jumps out, everyone clambers into the morning air, limping and stooped young men help each other out of cars, reluctant to leave the fragrance of gasoline and leather. They stand together in the parking lot, and just as the sun kisses the Golden Boy, there's the sound of hammering, it comes from the Legislative grounds. The parade wanders toward the noise.

Someone has wrapped a Union Jack around the front of the building, and as the vets' parade limps toward the gigantic flag, the well-dressed carpenters fall silent, bend at the knee to lift a wooden structure, 100 feet across, 25 feet deep. The astonished carpenters cheer wildly as the vast stage fits the stone steps, hugging the two bronze buffaloes. It is going to be a grand show.

Mary drops behind. She has forgotten her shoes, and her feet are burning. Jimmy Dunn, looking back at her, lifts one crutch in salute. As they cross Broadway, pink in the summer dawn, there's the skirl of a single bagpipe; the grieving piper, in his kilt on the vast stage, beckons. But Jimmy Dunn looks back at Mary who seems to have lost her wind, gone astray. Dunn says, "But I thought we were going to Victoria Park." "Dunn!" yells Bill, "get a move on!" Mary, forlorn.

left behind, can see the vets gathered beneath the stage. They lift their eyes to the Mayor who has a megaphone, his bewildering speech sliding on the dewy breeze.

Mary sits in Drinkwater's car. Nothing to do. Wonders vaguely what's going on at this Victoria Park, wonders what Eleanor is doing today. She's worried about getting back home and up to her room without getting caught. What if her father sees her driving with Drinkwater back down Broadway in the broad daylight? Oh hurry up Drinkwater with your damn trickery, because that's what it is, Mary knows it, all by herself in this damn car. Tricking those nice soldiers into thinking this is a Real Parade! DW can be a horse's ass when he wants to.

Hear them calling you and me
Every son of liberty.

But here is DW at last, pleased as punch that they fell for it, poor men, standing there in front of that stage with the Mayor going on about the Constitution. Drinkwater is removing his jacket, warm already. The wind from the south. Mary hears the Mayor say, *"It is like a drink of new wine to witness such expressions of loyalty."* And Mary wonders, *new* wine? She slouches in her seat, better down here, out of the wind, and her father won't see her if he does happen to go to the office early.

Drinkwater drives her home. Halfway there, she realizes they haven't spoken or looked at one another, not once.

These moments must be endured. Endure.

TO HELL WITH THE ALIEN ENEMY
GOD SAVE THE KING!

This is no lone piper, this is a whole brigade, this is a parade! Sir Rodney ignores the noise till he has finished his coffee, sits at the dining-room table longer than usual. *A sense of perspective is oc-casionally a sense of timing; things will be more coherent to me in ratio with the impetuosity of my approach to it.* But the drummers have learned another rhythm, quick and compelling even to Sir Rodney, who wipes his narrow mouth and calls for Mary as he opens his front door. *Of all the brazen foolhardy, what are those boys doing in this end of town?*

Sir Rodney, walking down the driveway, calling Mary, and the rest of the household emerging to follow him. And there, marching down the centre boulevard of Wellington Crescent, stepping blithely behind the old flag, The Boys of the Old Red Patch, these ones all in one piece, all of one mind, marching at ease to the roll of the drum. The household is there on the front lawn, and Sir Rodney walking slowly down the driveway. Mary appears from around back. She won't kiss her old father good morning. She won't meet his eyes.

So these are the ones on Our Side, and here we all are. They wear their cause more casually. They are singing.

i saw my buddies true
marching two by two
i saw one-legged pals
coming home to their gals

in my dream i saw

millions of soldiers
millions of men
millions of bullets
thundering past
millions of bodies
wounded and gashed

in my dream i saw

valleys of ruins
mountains of mud
beautiful rivers
rivers of blood

in my dream
of the big
parade

166

Helen

THE PLACE SEEMS DESERTED. It's haunted by the newcarpet steam-engine hotel smell, the departures of countless guests for their singular destinations. The young girl working Reception greets Eleanor with ancient forbearance and begins to explain, no staff, no rooms. But Eleanor tells her Helen said to come, so she's shown the swinging doors to the hotel dining room. Where 200 people pluck the meat off 200 soup bones, sip the broth and vacate their chairs for another 200. Between the long tables women in white aprons, their heads tied up with white kerchiefs, waltz through with nut-coloured wicker baskets full of torn loaves.

As Eleanor walks down the far side of the room a woman pockets the rest of her bread and hurriedly rises to offer Eleanor her place. "No," says Eleanor, and touches her arm, but the woman is so eager to give something, to get something back, and her eagerness is a little brown bird escaped from a cat. Eleanor is careful not to see another face, as she gathers her big purse to her stomach and makes for the kitchen door.

The noise in the dining room was cautious and sparse, but the kitchen is full of gratuitous laughter. Cooking pots clatter and the clash of a thousand spoons and half-a-dozen women working and talking nonstop. No one sees her, everyone looking up at her and smiling and they all carry on with their furious cooking. She chooses to situate herself, puts her purse behind a chair, rolls up the sleeves of her navy blue blouse. (She'd had to dress *casually* in front of her mirror, all the time grateful no one could see her.) And finally she has measured a teaspoon of space for herself, and loudly she asks them for Helen who sent her.

"Helen you want?"

"Why, I don't know."

"She's still in jail."

"No. She got out."

"No she never. They wouldn't give bail, the bastards."

"Watch your tongue!" And another shock of laughter.

They appraise her carefully (they know all about the mirror), and an older woman who is weary and hoping Eleanor is here to relieve her says, "No dears, Helen's been out since last night, I know, she was here early this morning when we served up breakfast." Facing Eleanor, this woman who is not much older but tired and quite beautiful, she is, a woman entirely without apologies. She is removing her apron and ties it at the back for Eleanor, then she shows her the makings for the next batch of soup. Celery, chop it fine, and the onions are done thank heavens for that.

So begins Eleanor's shift in the kitchen. She peels the carrots, like arthritic fingers, into the yellow basin, and chops them with a brutal little cleaver upon a wood cutting-board. And the carrots pile up into carrot-smelling discs or suns and Eleanor's hands are stained orange except for a single red cut where she looked up once.

And Sometimes Food Isn't a Metaphor

She's working like that, all but ignored by the others, listening to the strike-gossip, amazed to see Stevie flash through, *even here!*, when a lull in the conversation causes her to stop. From the unbolted delivery doors at the back there arrives a sizable woman with a coat, in this heat, slung over her shoulders. She is carrying a splintered crate brim-full of potatoes. Eleanor is closest; she tries to take half the weight from her, and together they ease the crate onto the big table in the centre of the kitchen. The woman grins at her and goes back to the lane for more.

"Well. I guess she's out."

So this is Helen Armstrong. And Eleanor figures she has been slicing vegetables long enough to merit an answer so she asks them what she was *in* for. Everybody has a different opinion on that. She was giving it hell at the Square and the Specials grabbed her for *disorderly conduct*. She attacked a scab newsie on Carlton selling the Trib. She *incited* Ida Kraatz and Margaret Steinhauer to attack *two* newsies selling the Free Press on Carlton. They charged her with *rioting*. They charged her with *intimidation*. They charged her with *unlawful assembly*. At any rate, they wouldn't grant bail, not for $1,000, not for $2,000. So she's been *in* for two, three days. That's Helen for you. Glad she's back. And when Helen reappears with the next load, there are many hands to help her.

The history
of all hitherto existing society
is the history
of class struggles

HERE. HAVE A CIGAR. Today's a day for the History Books, yessir. Here.
I'll light it for you. Yessireesir, and it's about time too, we showed
those Reds who's running this country, them or Constituted
Authority. By God we know how to pull together for the sake of the
Dominion, bless her heart.

> The King asked
> The Queen, and
> The Queen asked
> The Dairymaid:
> "Isn't there a quicker way
> To get rid of the Reds?"

Like a bullet, like a bomb dropped from the sky in the night.
Three readings in the House of Commons, three readings in the
Senate, and the unqualified approval of the Governor-General.

modern bourgeois society
that has sprouted
from the ruins
of feudal society
has not done away with

Gentlemen. It is late and we are all tired. We have worked hard tonight. I think it safe to aver, this evening there is no one in Canada could rightly argue that we have not earned our keep.

FORTY-MINUTE LEGISLATION

I'm grateful to all of you, for your bold vision, your forthrightness in dealing with this divisive issue. And so it gives me great pleasure to inform you, The Right Honourable Governor-General of Canada has given final approval to the amendment to the Immigration Act. (ripple of applause)

Any person deemed to be a revolutionary who was born outside of Canada, whether a British subject or a naturalized Canadian, will be summarily shipped back to the land of his birth.

May I propose a toast.

DEPORT THE ENEMY ALIEN!

And Senator Robertson says, "Hear Hear," and consults with General Ketchen. And General Ketchen says, "Well done! We'll ship them to Kapuskasing." But the Senator and the General confer with A.J. A—, K.C., and he hits on a better plan.

> *the bourgeoisie*
> *has drowned*
> *heavenly ecstasies of religious*
> *fervour,*
> *in the icy water*
> *of egotistical*
> *calculation. It has*
> *resolved personal worth*

into exchange value. In a used bookstore in Winnipeg, a man is chewing on an unlit pipe and reading, late, late into the night, into the small hours of the morning.

all that is solid
melts into air
all that is holy
is profaned, and man
compelled   to face
his real conditions
his mutual relations
with sober eye.

And outside the bookstore, on the empty street blown by a dusty nightwind, someone is leaning against a car. See his lean face under his hat. Watching.

91   10 gauge shot guns 35   snider rifles 26   revolvers 3
machine guns 3   officers 2   drivers 6   riflemen 2   mob
ile militia 1   troop Fort Garry Horse 1   motor machine gun

Rev. J.S. Woodsworth, son of Dr. James Woodsworth came all the way from Vancouver and addressed the Bolsheviks last night at the Labour Temple. His mother and his brothers, sisters and family are feeling keenly his attitude. It is a sad thing that the Bolsheviks are supported by three Methodist ministers.

I expect that the strike will be over this week and the streetcars running again. We may have a small riot or two before that, but these will end very quickly, as we are ready for them. Any impartial observer studying the whole situation would naturally come to the conclusion that a revolution was contemplated for the whole Dominion and that it was to begin at Winnipeg.

Thank God	*Civic*	*our Dominion*
our	*Firm*	*except aliens*
Governments	*Citizens*	*and Bolsheviks*
firm citizens		

From the diary of the Rev. Dr. John Maclean

section 2   guns infantry escorts   1 company motorized
infantry 1   mobile militia unit 1   troop Fort Garry Horse 1
motor machine gun section 2   guns infantry escorts 1   comp
any motorized infantry 272   men 10   officers 62 horses tot

The Strike is developing into a social revolution. The Bolshevik leaders intend to divide the country among themselves and their followers.

The Free Press

Strikers' Tuesday

Y*OU GET A VIEW FROM A HORSE, kind of gives you a better perspective. And our horses together, they make an awful sound on the streets, at a fast walk, couple of hundred of us, riding. In our hands, the good feel of a wood bat, sawed-off neckyoke, spoke of a wagon-wheel, heavy enough, neck rein, loose, and my other hand on the club, swing it gently beside my leg.*

We move down Rupert this way, just nice you know, just a walk but quick. Now's my chance, now's my chance to show somebody. And Pete Johnson beside me, not so good with his horse. The way he sits he's going over first sight of a gallop. But he likes this too, see him rub the club against his thigh.

Walter is standing in front of a men's clothing store when somebody, a guy he used to know, takes one of the Specials' clubs and throws it through the big window. It's Jacob, nice man, three kids, Jacob looking with regret at the glass splashed all over the quiet rolls of tweed and hound's-tooth, and tears in his eyes. Walter hates seeing Jacob crying; he seizes his face between his hands and shakes him out of it. Jacob crying and laughing, arms around each other, they move drunkenly out onto the street, then they're separated in the crowd.

Some fool tries to drive his car down Portage. It's surrounded by the Specials who have managed to stay on their horses, still swinging. Walter running to dodge one of them falls over somebody lying facedown by the side of the road. Lots of the horses riderless running wild, one of them dragging a man in its stirrup.

Then Walter sees him. MacDougal in a shirt, bloodied, but calm; that's euphoria on the man's face, Walter has seen it in the war, some guys come alive, times like these. MacDougal yelling into people's faces, Go Home, Go On Home, Clear out of here. By name, he tells them, Go home DaveJosephMichaelAdolphKarlJohnJennyAlfred

SPECIAL POLICE DRIVEN FROM THE STREETS!!

From an open window above the billboard for Sir Rodney Trotter's meat packers, SWEET CLOVER BACON & PORK SAUSAGE, a photographer leaning out, holding his heavy camera away from himself (the camera, distinct, the camera, still), white panama hats, only one woman and she is wearing—why does this matter?—a broadbrimmed hat, a long black skirt. The camera catching the movement of horses riding into the crowd, men stand to watch, men pushing others shoving, commotion scratches the camera's silver eye.

And now, how many minutes have passed before Walter becomes aware, before MacDougal wakes in the lull of soundwaves, and there are no Specials to be seen. Acting-Chief Major Lyle remembers a promise and orders the Specials off the streets. The fight is over, the Strikers will say they've won. The Specials have retreated to the Rupert Street Police Station.

Forever after Bobby Russell looks for a mysteryman by the name of Major Lyle. The story goes:

Russell and others from the Strike Committee are at Mayor

175

Gray's office to talk him out of putting the Specials on the streets. They're not having much luck, when out of nowhere walks this decentlooking fellow. He says, "Boys, I wish to have you come to my office, if you have time. I want your advice."

Well, you could knock Bobby over with a feather; these "Boys" are accustomed to abuse from official types by now. But no. This Major Lyle, a man in uniform, he says, "Come into my office, Boys. I want your advice." And the Strike Committee knows just what to tell him. Get the Specials off the street, or there'll be trouble. And take away the damn clubs.

So this Major Lyle, he says, "Excuse me, I wish to use the telephone." And he's only gone a minute, but when he comes back he apologizes again, for keeping the Gentlemen waiting. Then he says, "What else can I do for you?" You can bet your life, the Strike delegation tells him, Don't let the fools carry arms, because they're so nervous, they're going to shoot each other.

Then they shake hands and say Au Revoir and the Boys are walking on air.

Where is Major Lyle?

I received $210.00 for transportation and another $100.00 for travelling expenses. A Major Lyle was placed in charge of the 'Specials'. Certain of his actions were embarrassing to the Crown and on the 17th, it became necessary to send him out of the City. It was thought that to dismiss him could have a bad effect, so he was sent to Minneapolis on untenable business.

Sincerely,
I remain,

A. A— , K.C.

Golf

At the time of writing, Sergeant Fred Coppin, Victoria Cross hero of France, is lying in the Military Hospital and is stated to be dying. He is not expected to live until morning. Sergeant Coppin swears that his injuries were caused by three Austrians who kicked him in front of Alloway and Champion's offices on Main Street during the riot.

By the time that this appears, Coppin may be dead. Whether he is dead or alive; whether he lives or dies, the fact remains that he was kicked with intent to kill, by three Austrians—men whose blood relations he and every other returned fighter fought in France.

The Winnipeg Citizen

"So DID HE DIE?" asks Mary, smiling her indulgent smile, waiting for the punch line. "I think that's hysterical. Our British hero makes it through the whole bloody war and then gets kicked in the head on Main Street. What'd he do, fall off his horse?"

"Yes," says Drinkwater, "but the Bolsheviks were hurling stones."

"How awful," murmurs Melissa McQueen.

Mary's father puts his arm around Melissa as he hands his 5 iron to the caddy. "Troubled times indeed, my dear. A revolution," he says, as he approaches the next shot, just to the right of the green, a 9 iron should put her in nicely. "A Bolsheviki revolution, ahhhhh," chips the ball high and it rolls within an easy putt for 4 on the 7th hole, par. "The misguided alien. It was Prussian boots put to that poor soldier's head. And in some respects, it serves us right."

Sir Rodney Armstrong waits respectfully while the young Drinkwater takes his putt, a long and difficult shot which runs too fast over the dry green, past the hole, misses it by four inches and rolls another five feet. Young Drinkwater has a terrible temper when he's not playing well; the company watch him closely. He abuses himself when he plays bad golf, he hits at his shins with his putter, throws golfballs against his own forehead, has bitten his arm till it bled already this season. Mary is impatient with Drinkwater when he is like this. She wishes that she and Melissa had remained at the clubhouse. DW's tassled golf shoes are fascinating and utterly repellent. Why do men love to be watched at their tedious games, wearing their ridiculous sports-togs in this heat, trying to hit the little ball into the little hole with the big stick?

Drinkwater sinks his putt. Rodney resumes: "Yes, it serves us right. The immigrants have provided us with labour these past two decades and more. Yet, they are unruly, and in their ignorance they favour the radical solution. Bloodshed where there should be British liberty, fanatical terrorism where constituted authority rightly belongs. Anarchy and mayhem—here!" He waves his thin arms above his head, a generous gesture which includes the entire south nine, even extends as far as the river, barely seen now through the new leaves.

"But Sir Rodney." Melissa's interruption. "Excuse me, but my father told me the strike leaders are British."

"So they are, my dear," Rodney solemnly agrees, "and an egregious blight upon the moral principles of the law-abiding British citizen. But this Bolsheviki atheism is Russian, it originated in Russia and should be returned there before it destroys everything constitutional."

He places his ball firmly on the tee and takes a slow and determined practice swing with his driver. Somewhere a dove is hidden in the cool trees. Then, the clean percussion of a ball well hit; Rodney drives it straight down the fairway. "Nice shot!" says Drinkwater, too enthusiastic, and rushes his drive, slicing into the woods. "Perdition!" says Drinkwater, and hits himself with his driver.

Mary takes the club from Drinkwater and returns it to the caddy who follows discreetly several yards behind the loving couple as they fox-trot down the fairway. Mary joins Drinkwater in the woods to search for the ball. She finds one, but it's not his, it's dirty and has a smile on it whereas Drinkwater's balls are monogrammed. Mary is grateful to be in the shade, and with her back to the sunny fairway, she lifts her long skirt almost to her knees and fans her damp thighs. She is so tired of DW's need to impress her father. She despises a *needy* man. Thank God they are only playing nine holes and they can go back to the clubhouse and eat cucumber sandwiches on that nice bread. She knows DW has left a good Chablis in the cooler—it's a damn good thing her father has been able to supply the clubhouse with ice during this irritating strike.

"What are you two doing in there? Practising?" Melissa calls from the overexposed lawn, shading her eyes to peer into the woods. Strange. Melissa has become unbearably Witty of late; she has adopted this rakish personality. She's even taken to wearing shorter skirts. And she has cut off her hair in a vulgar sort of bob. When you really look, you can see, Melissa is panicky. Right now she is laughing hysterically at her own pathetic joke.

"I can't find my bloody ball." Drinkwater's nasal complaint.

"Hit another one from the fairway," calls Rodney, generous always. "It's just one shot." Then *sotto voce* to Melissa, "He's a good boy. But he must acquire the ability to relax."

After lunch, a late lunch that will have to see them to a late dinner, Drinkwater invites his fiancée to walk through the garden. Many years later, thinking back on that fateful day, Mary will ask herself why she succumbed, what was it, that particular day, June 11th, 1919, that led her to abandon all moral goodness, all the sweet refinement of her dear mother's memory? Then, but not now, she will know: it was his voice, definitely Drinkwater's voice. He says, "Let's go out to the garden." So she does, and they speak there, they really speak. It is wonderful.

It is afternoon, a green one. Such a dance never played in that garden. It is like Quebec, those cedar forests on the granite. It is like B.C., those rain forests, only much tidier. The riverbank has been cultivated, so lush, and he walks with her, she wearing that long skirt, soft cotton, robin's-egg-blue, it makes a breathing sound, an in and out sound. It is so close they are self-conscious, it is entirely different from the rest of the world.

He is telling her, he has been disappointed that he never served in the war. This is rare. What is also rare, increasingly in the years of their long marriage, is Drinkwater's confidence as he speaks. He is usually nervous and eager to please, but this afternoon he speaks soft against Mary's throat, lips moving words and kisses in her hair where it falls at the nape of her neck.

Do people still speak like that?

Do they know such long sentences not even run-on? Do they work thoughts into syntactical units of such breadth and complexity, using many thats and whichs, ors and not less thans? Equally, do they balance nouns with modifiers which in themselves do on occasion bring the reader to the fourth generation of a woman or a man before returning to the verb, a yearning form of to be, a would have, and sometimes an acquiesce? Verbs, so dangerously subjunctive, yield to prepositions enamoured of the passive voice. Yet, there is a noun, an object of intensity, of greatness, of courageous spirit; triadic nouns, even as they approach that semantic culmination which is the privilege of the transitional sentence, do not go beyond the natural restraint preserved for our use by our forefathers, ( ), whose love for the English language (lang. of the isle etc.) prevents the descent and fracture of idiom.

An Angel

Mary would be an admirable woman; her nature has been twisted from its natural shape by the savagery of the war and the upheavals at home. A young woman alone with a young man on property so carefully designed as to waver between garden and bush, on an evening in that month which is in itself transitional, a young woman of family with connections which, *though not exactly aristocratic, are unquestionably 'good'*, alone with a young gentleman who is nearly graceful, possessed of such a honeyed tongue, it seems, this afternoon, and she cannot help but yield to the persuasions of the moment, fleeting and transitory and fatal. They walk to the riverbank, sit on the hot green grass, Mary is trembling, Drinkwater leans over her, kissing and talking and kissing, he touches her legs, beneath her long skirt his hand moving like thirst on water, and nothing to prevent the warm hand from finding her and discovering the places she didn't even know herself and she is water filling those luxurious places, she opens and takes him and this is how it is, Mary and Drinkwater conceive the son and heir, their first born, conceived on the afternoon the Citizens' Specials ride through Market Square.

Here come the lovers, full of joy and mirth.
Joy, gentle friends! Joy and fresh days of love
Accompany your hearts!

WHEN DOES A WEDDING DAY BEGIN? In the dark, before the summer sunrise? In the dark, the young woman, who hasn't slept, who will not sleep, throws off the covers, rocking herself, caressing the pleasant chill of her own bare shoulder, caressed by the pale silk of her nightgown. Mary in her chamber, eyes open in the black-eyed day, *round the purple core*, her wedding day. Mary in the whispering dark, wondering, when does a woman become a wife?

Near her, she knows they are there, the unwrapped blue boxes in their rustle of tissue paper, the silver tea service, Queen Anne flatwear, one silver chafing dish, two charming silver vases perfect for pansies, six unaffected candlesticks and one complicated candelabra, graceful silver entrée dishes and hollow wear. The bride has chosen Doulton, bone, with a simple rose-and-lily pattern, gold. A hand-embroidered linen tablecloth with 12 silk-stitched runners and matching linery. Bedding, white, with pink needlepoint roses upon the pillowcases, plaited edges, lace.

Glassware, fine cut glass, ice-like, water goblets, wine glasses, a cream pitcher, fruit cups and summer salad bowls. Egg coddlers and snifters, porringers, peppermills and tiny spoons for salt. Painted figurines, "Fair Maiden," fresh and coy, in an apple-green dress and crinoline. Another, much larger, "My Love," womanly, mature, white dress white skin, offering a red rose.

Grateful, Meg has discovered a breeze; it breathes through the sleeping porch where she and her husband are lying in the sticky heat. Lying so still, they each think the other is sleeping, listening to their own restless children telling dreams in their sleep. But the noises, Meg wakes fully to this, the voices are coming from outside. She rises on one elbow to lift the curtain, and there in their back yard, dozens of Specials, and Mounties. She turns to Bob and whispers into his ear, "Don't speak out loud. They're in the back yard dear, police, the Red Coats, lots of them. What will we do?" By now, they are banging on the front door. "Open, or we'll break it." And the children are awake and crying. Meg says, "Go away. You can't come in here. The children are asleep." Bob Russell opening the door to them, Chief Newton walking in and saying, "I'm sorry it had to be you."

Dear Diary

The dawn is magnificent, oh hell. Eleanor, woken early by the sound of traffic, Strange, before it is quite light. She climbs out to the roof, tears her gown on the windowsill. This must be a perfect time to write, these odd hours, let the owl speak, let me say something to this page. She is wondering; a style ornate and full of trickery has always been desirable, till of late. She would like to say it today with words solitary, one, among many. But today, Mary is marrying Drinkwater and I am her Maid of Honour and my words must be kind and tailored to meet Mary's needs, her cup which runneth over with dry champagne.

To lose oneself so completely to sleep, to dream in colour, this is a rare and wonderful event. MacDougal lying in the muskeg of deepest sleep, dreaming of Eleanor's ebony piano, and even in sleep, his other voice's commentary, Ahh I am having a dream of Eleanor's ebony piano, and the colours are Chopin's, gold soap chiaroscuro velvet, but why in God's name would anyone wake me from such exotic travel?

And MacDougal finally pulled from unstill waters by the raucous banging on the front door of his shop below. He can't put his head out the window because the screens are on, but he calls through, politely as a man hoping to return to innocence. "I'm here," he says, "what do you want?"

Someone says his name. "Yes," says MacDougal, "that's me." They have a warrant for his arrest. He must come downstairs at once. MacDougal pulling on a shirt and trousers in front of the window notices the cars on the street, motors running, headlights out, and on the sidewalk, dozens of cops and several Mounties.

They take him to the northend station. They take all of them there, Bray, Armstrong and Ivens, Heaps and Queen. And they've picked up half a dozen men with foreign-sounding names, for good measure. Word is, they're going to be on a train east in a couple of hours and on a ship overseas by tonight. But somebody gets uneasy about the public reaction to this. So while day seeps in, they put them all back into the cars and drive them out to Stony Mountain. The Warden there is a bit confused. He has never received prisoners before who haven't yet been convicted of any crime. But it all works out in the end: the Minister of Immigration gets up early and sends a very official authorization.

Better Late Than Never

Notwithstanding any doubts I have as to the technical legality of the arrests and detention at Stony Mountain, I feel rapid deportation is the best course now that the arrests are made, and later we can consider ratifications.
(Sir A. M— , Minister of Interior, telegram to A. A— , K.C.)

Voice Lessons

When the magic dawn dries up into another hot morning, and Eleanor still hasn't written the words that will let her out of Mary's wedding day, she wants to put a call in to MacDougal to tell him, I love you. Then she will love him and that will make it true. That will make the borrowed-and-blue of Mary's $10,000 wedding a harmless bit of theatre, a character-part. It is a question of dexterity. Eleanor will love MacDougal, she'll live in that love like the rest of her life has been nothing but training in theatre, in movement. And every word she has ever uttered before she utters I-love-you to MacDougal will be nothing but singing lessons, exercises for diaphragmatic breathing. Every sound she has ever formed will be kissed away to the land of Story to be reshaped by the ironic gestures of mythic creatures whose names she can't remember.

MacDougal I love you and today I am being driven to Westminster Church in a baby-blue Packard. It's a conspiracy, MacDougal, but I am just a spy. But then she must dress in the satin and the sequins and the diamond necklace, an heirloom, and she is taller than ever in the off-white shoes and she sees in the mirror that she is her own double agent. And when from the window of her elaborate lair she sees the big car pull up to collect her, she quickly places the call to MacDougal which will send such a ripple through the set it might tear the scenery. But there is no answer. MacDougal isn't home.

Epithalamion
Mary in the bath in a mist

The big bathtub has brass claws like lions' paws. Studying them, Mary, sitting in the white chair, in a white towel, motionless.

But it is getting late. The wedding is at two. There is much to do to Mary before then. Her hair must be combed and plaited in a modest roll, loose, so that little pieces will stray to her throat. That is just the beginning. Think of the hands, the feet, and the powdery down in the small of her back. Mary must be prepared to be wed to young Drinkwater.

Her dress is perfection. Traditional, yet with that inimitable distinction of style that is Mary's own. It is astonishing. You see her, the bride, in veil and lace, so modest, so chaste. Yet, yet, surely you are mistaken but isn't there just that trace of seduction, the lace has fallen, been replaced, just so.

She scorns the ancient superstition that the bride must not be seen before the ceremony. And her father (for whom this day becomes a distillation of his own moments of love), her doting and somewhat confused father has allowed for this breach of ritual. There is a luncheon—not much to speak of, hors d'oeuvres, a glass between friends. Fifty happy young people dressed to the nines.

Then they all depart for the church and the polliniferous dusky smell of champagne and roses accompanies them through the sunny streets. Laughter, much laughter, everyone sparkles, and the bubbles of wit carry them from their cars and up the stairs to the carpeted vestibule to the aisle to the curved wooden pews to witness this sacred nuptial, the wedding of Mary to Drinkwater, I do.

In the interlude while Mary and Drinkwater are in the Reverend's office to sign the Register, Melissa McQueen wants to move from her place beside Todd to a spot beside Jeremy but she falls off her high heel right in the middle of the aisle, and that is so funny (Melissa handles it awfully well, anyone else would die), the entire wedding party is chuckling except for Frances Matheson who is laughing hysterically. When Mary and Drinkwater and the Minister return from signing the Register, everyone but Frances manages to be quiet, but Reverend Christie isn't amused and before he pronounces Mary and Drinkwater Man and Wife, he scolds the youthful gathering for their delinquent behaviour.

There aren't many men in the Labour Temple today. Word of the arrests has been slow to reach the Strike Committee. Helen finally organizes the wives who have had to find babysitters and collect their wits, calming their children and the grandparents who are so frightened there are moments when they wonder if their grown children could possibly be guilty, though no one thinks this long enough to say it. And there are only a few men in the offices of the Ukrainian Labour Temple and the Labour News. No one can positively say that the raids were carried out simultaneously. But sometime during the afternoon, a handful of Specials enters each of these places and empties every cupboard, drawer, and closet onto the floor, breaking anything that is locked, smashing open anything that looks purposively closed. The entire place and the contents therein, every shred of human activity counts as evidence of Revolutionary activity, every word written and echoing, Sedition, Conspiracy, utterly foreign to any law-abiding citizen.

And while Helen is right to keep the girls active, involved, distracted, it means that they are not at home when the Mounties get there. And so for the children of the *Reds* who are now sitting in Stony Mountain Penitentiary, it is a trauma so unimaginable as to falter on the steps of their memory, and it will repeat itself over and over like the tripped needle on a phonograph. When the wives of the prisoners return to their homes late tonight, in the dizzying uncertainty of the future, they will find that the living room, the kitchen, the spare room, their bedrooms, the shed, have been broken. The letters have been stolen. The private letters are not private, the voices have been taken, their lives have been confiscated, and the intricate conversation, the dreams they have been telling one another in the night have become *evidence, a conspiracy*. Scattered.

Sir Rodney's Splendid Surprise

They are gathered, if such can be said of a crowd like a rampant garden wildly astray, they are gathered in the solarium. It is terribly

187

hot in here. It has been a day of romance. They have eaten lightly, but well. They have sipped, supped, and tonight, they will dance. This is the wedding of the year, of the decade.

The friends of the newly married couple have arranged for a swing band at the Fort Garry and they have collected their wraps, ready to dance through the brief summer night. But before he lets the young people go, Sir Rodney has something to say, it won't take long, bear with me, I am cognizant of the irrepressible nature of your joy. And so well-bred are they, and such is their gratitude for the long rhythms of this wedding day, they do indeed stop for a moment in the solarium and listen to Sir Rodney speak his few words to a departing daughter, an only child.

Mary is at one side, Drinkwater at the other, Sir Rodney holding each by the hand. Sir Rodney is so elegant in his grey morning coat, Mary bites her lip. Her father has tears in his eyes but his voice is steady, and he says, "You all know, this young woman is the light of my life. Since her mother died, I must confess, I have relied upon her as my only source of happiness. It has been perhaps too much a burden." (Mary murmurs, "No.") "But there it is, the simple truth." He puts his arm around Drinkwater now, and he says, "I thought I would die too, if I were to lose her. But today, I welcome into our home and into my affections, a young man of such fine character and of such generous enthusiasms, I am convinced that their love will breathe new life into my old one."

A sprinkling of applause, tears, Melissa puts her glass down. Sir Rodney holds Mary's, Drinkwater's, hands before him. He continues. "Mary. Son. I am a selfish old man. I want to keep you, and I know I must let you go. But it is my rather desperate wish to keep you within my arms' reach."

With this, Sir Rodney nods to a servant who has been standing at the entrance to the room. The servant turns off the lights. The solarium is dark, the street is dark, and beyond, just across the street, the delighted company see a grand house lit up like a ship, gorgeous, remote. Mary looks at him with astonishment. Sir

Rodney barely touches her face, tenderly, secretively, as someone touches a too-lovely painting in a gallery.

"I bought it for the two of you. If you will accept it, I give it to you with all the affection of a father's heart."

It is nearly too much. They embrace, Mary and her father, for a long time. Drinkwater stands with his back to his party, staring in amazement at the great house across the street. He is trying to figure out how the old man arranged it. He and Mary have already bought the Suckling house on Cambridge. Sir Rodney must have fixed it up with Tom Suckling. The old fox. Think of that. What an amazing guy.

They remain standing in the darkened solarium while Sir Rodney turns, shyly, to his new son-in-law. They shake hands manfully. The gift has taken the swagger out of Drinkwater. He stands beside his new wife, *his new wife*, like two Drinkwaters. It's uncanny—his friends can see him change before their eyes. His little speech of gratitude, spoken with the voice of the old Drinkwater, ornately sober, sweet as amaretto, the voice which everyone had believed would resist sincerity as it would resist time itself. But this liquorish voice is wondering aloud, "How do I thank you? I have always found it difficult to speak my feelings, gratitude being especially difficult to put into words." He waves vaguely to his young friends. "But how do I thank you for a gift so—so generous?" His laugh is actually self-deprecating. "How does one thank you for a house?"

His bewilderment is real. Mary tips her head in a foolish sort of puppy-gesture watching him. Well, she has married someone, my god, she touches his arm, yes, Drinkwater is real, bigger than she remembers him, and not quite so convenient.

Dawn

THE COP ON THE CORNER has been instructed to leave her alone. They'd told him down at the station that she'd probably turn up and to keep his hands off her. She must be rich to get special attention like that. She sure looks rich.

The cop in his car on the corner sits, black on black, invisible, and he watches Eleanor drive up to MacDougal's bookstore. She just sort of slides out, she's in this slippery sort of dress, at least it looks slippery from here. He sees her wrap herself up in a frothy coat and step up to the bookstore like she's waiting for an invitation. She wavers on the sidewalk there.

The cop can easily see from his car, Eleanor hovering outside MacDougal's place. They'd told him she was nicelooking, but they were wrong. She's rich, that's all, too skinny, no tits.

Nobody had bothered to close the door of MacDougal's shop. Eleanor pushes it open, she sees the books and papers spread all over the place. She calls him, her hand running over the wall inside the front door seeking the light. Calls him again. She listens carefully. Across the street, the cop sees her close the door, she finds the lightswitch, he sees bits of her through the window, moving around in the lit bookstore.

MacDougal's handmade bookcases are empty. His desk has been

190

split open, everything spilt and torn. Catches some paper on her heel, walking through the shop to the stairs out back, and up to MacDougal's suite, all the time saying his name to fill up the space with it. His place has been turned inside out. She has never been in his flat before. She sees the little carpets flipped over and the mattress halfway on the floor and the small kitchen spilt out. She reverses these images; in her mind, she is putting everything back so she can see MacDougal's suite like it really looks. She is appalled at MacDougal's modesty. He hasn't been concealing anything after all. For the first time, Eleanor doubts her future with him. A man with no secrets might not be capable of love. She'll have to keep hidden this knowledge of him. She turns out the lights and finds her way back downstairs in the dark.

The booze, which Eleanor has sipped in splashes and trickles all day long, acts like a paintbrush, blurring the edges between the hours and Eleanor. It is important to close firmly the precarious door to her friend's bookstore. Madly, she tries to lock it with her car-key. By way of compromise, she closes it with all her long weight, presses the door closed for a minute on the assumption that the longer she closes it the more closed it will be.

She feels like she's driving an airplane. She is masterful at the wheel, and glad, because she knows the way to Helen Armstrong's house, MacDougal had once pointed it out to her. When she arrives, their house is awake and people are coming outside all in a rush. Eleanor gets out and stands swaying on the boulevard while Helen and a bunch of others come down the walk. Helen recognizes her and looks embarrassed, but maybe this is because she isn't used to giving that envious once-over to other women, and she does this simply because she hadn't realized that Eleanor is a rich girl, the times they have met before. Helen explains, there's a chance the men will be let out early this morning and they're all driving out to Stony Mountain to get them. Eleanor can follow them if she wants to come. So she does, and in this way, Eleanor learns of their release before she learns of their imprisonment.

They wait at the end of the road in the blue light of dawn. Cold and sober now, Eleanor waits in her car. She shouldn't be here, in her dance frock, like yesterday's beauty queen. The others huddle together and they are dressed for the day. Finally, they see the seven men walk out the penitentiary gate, toward the cars waiting for them outside the walls. Queens, Heaps, Ivens, Armstrong, Bray, Russell, and MacDougal, see his white shirt in the cinematic light. He doesn't notice Eleanor's car, and stands with everyone together while a basket of food is brought out, and a quiet celebration begins. The sky is turning red. Eleanor waits while they have their meal. When it is apparent they are ready to go, she gets out and calls MacDougal's name. He does not look happy to see her. But he waves to the others, and weary, he comes to her car. She apologizes and touches his knee.

"Are you all right?"

"Yes of course." He glances back at the prison. "They didn't let the others out."

"Who's that?"

"Five more in there. Anyone with a zed in his name didn't get bail."

But did you see one man with a gun in the crowd?

WALTER'S KNEES ARE DUSTY, and his pants smell like rot, not an unpleasant smell after all, the degradation of matter, animal, vegetable, this hot summer upon us, gardens growing and rotting simultaneously; lowering himself over the tomato plants, disturbing their musty limbs, to shake the smell of them, and the weasels die and rot quick in the thick hedges. Walking, Walter smells dead meat in the bush, even in town, funny thing. And downtown, it's the garbage and the zooming flies, the yellow exhumations of citysmell.

Walter sits on the steps of Dingwall's Jeweller. This is a Silent Parade and Walter is Silent. He waits with his mates, fellow vets, they wait for their Soldiers' Committee, gone to talk to that wily bastard of a Senator, tell him to get the goddam streetcars off the streets. And along comes the Canon, the bag of wind, jolly as a flag. "Ah welcome Canon," Walter sighs, moves over to accommodate the Canon who is sitting himself down close as heat beside Walter on Dingwall's limestone steps.

"And we find ourselves once again, comrades in a war zone, Walter." The Canon likes to pick up conversation like a stillburning cigar. He snuggles against Walter, it nearly makes Walter crazy feeling him in this heat. The Canon is ecstatic though and there's no stopping him, downhill from here, he goes, "Walter. Old age has

193

had its day. It's the war that's done it. The young world must be run by young men."

Walter studies the Canon's grey lines, his thin face, his eloquent nose. Walter has learned much from the Canon. In France, the Canon had recited his poems,

> in the manner of Rupert Brooke,
> heavy with Greek

he'd say them in the trench just when the enemy attacked,

> the sting, the blinding shells, an orchestra,
> pompous as Beethoven,

and that's when Walter learned that the most ordinary people carry with them the most madness. Well-heeled, vigorously articulate, the Canon inflicts himself better than any one-legged shell-shocked poorboy. Respectable and banal to his long teeth, he fills the vast spaces rented by the Establishment, growing strange and wild things behind the sanctum.

"Come, let's join the lads," says the Canon. The vets are idling up to Main Street, left turn for City Hall. The Canon's bony grey fingers massage Walter's shoulder as he marches, school-boy, into the long line of men.

BLOODY SATURDAY

R.N.W.M.P. Make Gory Debut! Peaceful Citizens Shot Without Warning! City Under Military Control!

The pressure on Walter's shoulder increases. The Canon has started to sing, "Rock of Ages cleft for me, Let me hide myself in thee." Walter loves the Canon's voice, its timbre the warm interior of a church, glossy beams, bottled light. "Look out lad! It's begun!" Pulling Walter off the road, stumbling out of the way as 50 men ride through the crowd, they wear admirable shiny boots, khaki Specials. Main Street is very broad, with broad sidewalks filled with soldiers and men in civvies and a pretty woman holding a basket, strawsmell, lots of room for horses down the centre of Main, quickride, the

Silent Parade closes behind them. The police turn around at the Union Bank, ride back before the parade has a chance to give them room, so they are riding through the crowd. The Hissing and Booing frustrate the crowd so they chuck a few stones at the cops and that's better. Walter plucks a pair of those shiny boots, glad he is tugging at a man without spurs, gives a good pull. Sick with pity for the bloody little spitball he's pulled from his horse, loathes the ingratiating smile on the boy's face spinning and pinned to the road, kicks him one in the kidneys.

Chief Newton calls the Mayor who is in a room at the Royal Alexandra Hotel having an argument with three delegates from the pro-strike vets. Newton tells the Mayor the crowds outside are too big for the Specials to handle. Right away, the Mayor goes out (he takes the back lanes, the streets are full now, the noise, like the crashing surf *just beyond*), goes to the Mountie headquarters and asks Perry to send out his force. Perry dispatches 54 men on horses and 36 in trucks.

The biggest crowd is the one on Main, right around William and Rupert. When these people see the streetcar south-bound down Main, they move at it fast.

from the distance, a wave, flowing

They're so mad now, this kind of lover's passion in their faces. They're losing it, they want to lose themselves, they work toward this letting go, letting go. They press against the streetcar, haul it off the trolley and smash up the windows, they rock it rock it till it's nearly over. They go inside it they knife its seats rip it up and set fire to its insides it stinks of skin and rubber. The Mounties come now swinging down clubs in their hands. The crowd sings them a song of hate. Somebody jumps in front jigging his hat at the horse but these aren't Specials, these men can ride. Bricks in the air, stones and bottles. A horse catches a leg in the tornoff fender of the streetcar, throws its rider, drags him till a big guy hauls him off and punches him in the stomach. When the Mounties see this, they're quick, turn their horses around and pull out their guns.

From a balcony on City Hall,
the Mayor sees the guns.

He sees the guns and he figures he'd better read the Riot Act, get everybody off the streets. He turns to go inside. He hears shots. *They ran like rabbits.*

Shotshotshotshot getting shotshot on William Avenue, "They treated us worse than we ever treated Fritzy."

"Did they run?"
"Yes they ran fast."
"Did you shoot as they ran?"
"Yes, we were shooting as they ran."

And the Mayor, in his wisdom, had said that very morn, *"Any women taking part in today's parade, do so at their own risk."*

Shooting to Kill

The red-coats reined their horses and reformed opposite the old post office. Then, with revolvers drawn, they galloped down Main Street, and charged into the crowd on William Avenue, firing. One man, standing on the sidewalk, thought the Mounties were firing blank cartridges. Until a spectator standing beside him dropped with a bullet through his breast. Another standing nearby was shot through the head.

MacDougal is standing on the steps of the Manitoba Hotel. Eleanor stands beside him. They both see young Stevie across the street. They can hear shots on Main. MacDougal waves to him, *Go home Stevie*, he waves. Stevie smiles, like a flower in a battlefield, and walks across the street. It is as if the boy is enjoying the disruption, the men on the streets. He sees MacDougal waving to him, he goes to him. The Mounties come around from Main toward the hotel, firing into the air, into the crowd. Stevie, in the middle of the road, eager to receive a message from his friend this so-serious MacDougal. The bullet, the hot shell, in the boy's face, it shoots off the face, he falls.

MacDougal is already here, he cradles the boy in the middle of the street while the Mounties ride around the little scene.

MacDougal with the dead boy in his arms. Eleanor standing beside them, her empty arms waving, waving, waving.

The Canon is warming his skinny bum on the hot cobblestones. Everyone has gone home, except the red-coats, except the militia sitting in their cars with their machine guns, except a couple of Citizens who want to turn back. The city is quiet as a man with his hands up. He sees the blood blooming behind his eyelids, he lifts his face to the sun.

Deep in the ruined gardens of the Canon's mind

LIST OF ILLUSTRATIONS

Photograph #1.

The children are waiting. While they wait they make mud pies in the rain. In dust they simmer the long summers. Through the bones of the wood door lie the tracks of dust, or drifts of snow, answering the wind. And we wonder, How far have we come? My words are failures. They don't invent the house the lines of laundry the pockets of men the patient fingers of women measuring days in stitches. They don't invent the thin handsome woman holding her sick grand-daughter, her eyes looking back to the first utterance the first failed words. The children are waiting. Still.

Photograph #2.

These are theatrics. The necessity of writing is the necessity of asking you to move from the chair where you sit with your hands folded. You are young and tolerant, watching your sick husband's scant back, his blue bitten fingers under unwashed hair, his shirt you should wash but he won't let you have it because he can't sit up long enough to remove it. The necessity of asking your sick husband to get up, get up and let my own sick husband lie on the cot and stare at the patterns in the green wallpaper and sleep and I will watch over him, and you will have vanished. Vanquished. This is compassion. This is empathy. This is an entry.

Photograph #3.

I took this photograph. I have stolen the heavy scarf from around your hair (I guess that your hair is auburn because auburn is a colour that writes well). I take your sister, too, and the baby who finds the useful breast beneath so much rough homespun. Homespun is like auburn, a word my tongue knows, my fingers tell, the screen gives back to me, it says *homespun, auburn*. Your own round baby sits on your knee while you wait by the side of the road. Two small boys who haven't photographed well wander out of focus. I haven't a name for them, not auburn or homespun, but one boy looks *Mongolian*. I have taken you and your sister and your children and the sacks of your belongings, and the thin urn beside the leather trunk containing the things you've brought from *Mongolia. Urn.*

You and your sister are younger than I am now. You have been dead for 50 years. Bones, somewhere near me, grin the ancient grin. The sardonic bones are laughing, sophisticated, surprised by nothing, least of all the scandal of a word.

Photograph #4.

There is nowhere to put my things in your house. Your clock sits on the oil cloth (*oil cloth*) along with a glass bowl of sugar, a spoon, a silver shaker of salt, a tin plate squeezed by the damp tea towel. Evidence of a crime. The appearance of truth or reality.

There is nowhere for me to sit, your rooms are so crowded by the wood stove, its kindling, its kettle, the brother-in-law asleep on the cot, his undershirt clinging to the chipped bedpost. There is no place for me to stand where the floor doesn't buckle and tilt, where a penny won't roll crazily across the room to where you are standing in the curtained daylight with a boy. Your faces are shadowed by the light behind your back.

Photograph #5.

Parade: an aerial view from the *portico* of the Legislature, see the field of faces like a field of alfalfa or sunflowers, caps and collars and one man with his arm in a cast up to his elbow.

They swim, against waves of fear.

Photograph #6.

For those with a taste for contrast. Soft, against hard; the random, under control; the few, against the many. It is the photograph on the front page today. The familiar brutal erotic. Pentimento. A momento.